De Cero to Zero,
a Tale

De Cero to Zero, a Tale

Edel Romay

Library of Congress Control Number: 2021918039
ISBN: Hardcover   978-1-5065-3861-7
              Softcover   978-1-5065-3860-0
              eBook   978-1-5065-3859-4

Print information available on the last page.

Rev. date: 14/09/2021

To order additional copies of this book, please contact:
Palibrio
1663 Liberty Drive
Suite 200
Bloomington, IN 47403
Toll Free from the U.S.A 877.407.5847
Toll Free from Mexico 01.800.288.2243
Toll Free from Spain 900.866.949
From other International locations +1.812.671.9757
Fax: 01.812.355.1576
orders@palibrio.com
833577

I dedicate this work to my partner Anita Romay for placing her absolute trust in a dreamer like me.

ACKNOWLEDGEMENTS

My gratitude goes to all those authors, —dead or alive— I have read over the years. This work was also favored by Tiziana Laudato's artistic inspiration and intellectual discernment of the Spanish and English languages used in translating my manuscript.

CONTENTS

INTRODUCTION

How close is zero to zero?
—Robert Kaplan[1]

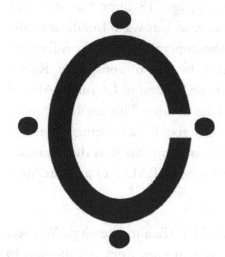

*I*t is a widely accepted fact that life on planet Earth is based on the carbon atom's capacity to share pairs of electrons with other carbon atoms to form covalent chemical bonds that organize the basis of organic life, including that of humans. I drew the well-known Lewis structure of the carbon atom to the left, which we owe to the American chemist Gilbert Newton Lewis and illustrates the dance of his four

---

1   Robert Kaplan: *The Nothing that is. A Natural History of Zero*, New York, New York: Oxford University Press (1999).

covalent electrons bond. Curiously inspired by the C of this carbon atom, I decided to give my stories the C's sequence.

Ninety-six percent of the human body comprises four elements — carbon, oxygen, hydrogen, and nitrogen—. The rest is an eclectic mixture of minerals and metals. But the paradox here is that the human being is animate. Despite being made up of 3×10^{36} inanimate particles, it has a soul. And this happens to humans, I insist, under carbon and its four covalent electrons that can bond to any substance, no matter how exotic.

On the other hand, reading is, in itself, an act of dialogue with the author, an act that I frequently perform. Some time ago, you saw, I conversed with Robert Kaplan while reading his book *The Nothing that Is. A Natural History of Zero*, when, on page 218, almost at the end, I heard the voice of Nāgārjuna, the master of *Mahāyāna* Buddhism, raise the following conjecture: «between the empty world and the full world, which would you choose?» To which, by way of conspiracy, Robert whispered in my ear: « Opposites are an illusion of language. All and nothing, as you know, are equally false nouns». This argument made me ponder: from 0^0 —that is 1— to 0, 1 goes back to being 1 —that is 0^0— Besides, human reality (Reality), as I consider it, is the boundary between the macro-reality of the universe (REALITY) and the inner nano reality of the atom (reality).

Do you follow? That is, [REALITY (Reality) reality]. You see, in the blink of an eye, the binary system goes from nothingness to everything, from 0 to 1, by which we might assume that human reality fluctuates between darkness and light: [Off-On]... And do not laugh; think about it; evidence of this is the entire electronic world that runs on binary code. Wait a minute!

—I remember; therefore, you exist —you assured me.
—I remember; therefore, I exist —I replied.
—Therefore, you and I exist at this moment —intervened my third "I" —between two tongues.

And so, it was that my multiple selves began to dialogue between two crepuscules:

En un cerrar y abrir de ojos,
universos nacen,
y universos mueren igualmente.

En un abrir y cerrar de ojos,
vamos de la luz a la oscuridad.

En un cerrar y abrir de ojos,
vamos de la oscuridad a la luz.

So, I heard myself tell you:

In a blink of an eye
universes are born,
and universes die too.

In a blink of an eye
we go from light to darkness.

In a blink of an eye
we go from darkness to light.

And this is how the symbiosis between author and reader is produced and reproduced. When this book reaches your hands, you and your other selves are going to bring it to life as you read. Of course, I am referring to the other, I mean, to you. You, the one who is connecting me with what I have already written. The time traveler. You, my other-self.

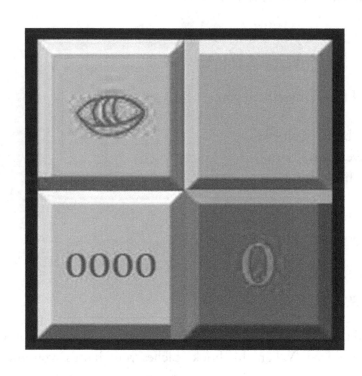

THE REFUGE

Narrative
©1998 Edel Romay

CURIOUS NOTE AS A
PRELIMINARY GUIDE

My other self-argued with itself, multiplying itself in its image: «To look back, to try to search through the labyrinths of memory for the truth of reality would be like searching for the reality of truth; in other words, an overly complex quest.» But I ask myself: «what is truly real in that which we call reality?»

For example, I am the other, this other who thinks of me. That which is reflected in me, that which lives in memory. Unlike those who are almost always in the present or, on occasion, in the future. All right! I am referring, without a doubt, to the one who is waiting for me to be him when you and I decide to reflect on ourselves in the mirror of the mind. In that case, you and I engage in the blissful inner dialogue of creation in one way or another. Or the external exchange of expression. Have you realized? In both cases, you and I are accomplices of the reflection. You, the other me who perceives me when he reads me. Do you hear me?

The genesis of the refuge

It arose when I was dialoguing about that landscape rescued from the memory of the other. The one that only looked into my eyes when I looked into the mirrors in the same way. Curiously, on one of those rare occasions, I was sure I had discovered him. «He too —I thought —had another "I" behind his face.» I surprised him, reflected in his gaze reflected in me. And I am pretty sure he had not realized. But let us continue; as I mentioned, we slowly descended along the rugged path that, step by step, led us to that well-known place where the very silence of the refuge welcomed us. We could almost guess the small, scattered sounds that turned into a melody with the wind's barely perceptible dancing on the trees' leaves. Suddenly, my thoughts were alerted when

I heard: «don't be surprised if, when we reach the pond, I observe absolute silence, I won't have left, I'm here and there simultaneously.» I think that is what the author told me when he disappeared through the labyrinths of memory

The sortilege of April 19, 1998

I conversed with Hamlet on the Holodeck in the dining room when the telephone rang quite unexpectedly halfway through reading. At that moment, I had a bad feeling, irrational, maybe, but genuine along the lines of a hunch. I got up from the table and walked towards the telephone. I hesitated for a moment, but I soon picked up the receiver. And oh, how bewildered I was to hear the voice of my friend in Mexico City announce the terrible news that Octavio Paz had died. I did not know what to say; I just about managed to hear a series of words floating in the void. It had been two months since I had called him, although it was not with him that I spoke, but with the person in charge of the house, who informed me that Mr. Octavio Paz was somewhat ill and that, aside from that, his library had burned down. Some news! And then that he physically left this world. I did not know what to do, and I could not do anything. And I did nothing; I only looked back at the book instinctively, and to my great surprise, saw Eliza Weizenbaum emerge from page 68 and greeted me with coquetry.

—Don't be surprised —she said. And I continued to listen to what I was reading.

—Long before the arrival of what is now referred to as multimedia, —I was advised by Dr. Murray —there was a space in the history of computers that demonstrated their narrative power with the same apprehensions of surprise and fear that Lumière's train had caused for the film camera. —Believe it! —Said Eliza smiling. At that moment, I realized that realities somehow intertwine. I closed the book and said to myself: "I'll go and investigate." I had to keep my mind busy. The news had touched me deeply.

Soon, I went to my library

And there I learned that, in 1966, Joseph Weizenbaum, a professor of cyber science at the Massachusetts Institute of Technology (MIT), created, as an experiment with the natural language of a processor, a program called Eliza, which could hold a conversation in the processor, answering with printed sentences. It occurred before the everyday use of screen computers (PCs). The program was an ingenious form of a Teletype connected to one of the first networks of timeshare computers. The result was surprising, paraphrasing patients' concerns as did psychologist Carl Rogers. According to Murray, Eliza also displayed a close Freudian interest in issues such as sex and family in this configuration. To Weizenbaum's distress, various people, including her secretary, "demanded" that they be allowed to talk to the system in private. Then they vehemently insisted that Eliza understood them despite Weizenbaum's objections and that her presence was real! That she resided somewhere in the system. Faced with this situation, Weizenbaum wrote: «even the most sophisticated users, although they are well aware that they are talking to a machine, soon forget this. Just as theatre spectators do when they reach the plot's suspense: they believe that what they are witnessing in the play is "real," Eliza claimed to be persuasively hallucinogenic. And just as the story of the Lumière train is a genre for the cinema's trajectory, so is the story of Eliza for cybernetics. In other words, Eliza is a legend». However, I talked with her for a few minutes, and you witnessed our conversation.

Finally, in May 1998

At the first attempt, I worked out the refuge's history with the total conviction that Eliza, somewhere in cyberspace, would be observing me and, in doing so, I would manifest myself in her Reality. And, in parallel, somewhere in the mental space, Octavio Paz would also manifest himself. All I was, was the connection between «here and there.»

IN NER SPACE: THE SCREEN LIGHTS UP

At 6ix in the afternoon

—Reality —the mind proposed.
—Which? —You questioned.
—The human one! —I exclaimed.

Thoughts materialize through words, and Imagination gives them physical form. But language is subject to the verb tense. That is right! The Reality, through language, seeks the possibility of being ignited. In other words, to make oneself intelligible. But Reality goes far beyond the simple declension of the verb.

—Don't confuse me. Reality is an accident of time —you established.
—In the darkness of the void, light is language ignited —I answered.
—Words are the Big Bang of understanding —you affirmed.

En algún lugar del cerebro

—On the question of Reality, what is Reality? —*Cuestionó la mente.*
—The intelligibility of time —*respondió la imagen.*
—Nothing is real without evidence —*dijiste tú.*
—Nothing is real without an observer —*te respondí yo.*

Vietnam, 1969

"If the world exists in our language —babbled Bach-Tuyet Tran, an 18-year-old Vietnamese girl —I'm willing to describe certain things that happen to us». And she continued to move away from the hamlet as she stroked a *cá* ('fish' in her language) between her fingers. In the distance, the bombs would continue to explode without respite. Bach-Tuyet continued, in the fog of the early morning, to move away from the farmhouse.

The pond of dreams

«*A* dyke reflected in the gaze of a salamander,» thought the *cá* inquisitively while surrounded by other amphibians. And the cá continued swimming glued to the surface of the pond, as the cá remembered being the image of a 25-year-old boy in the depths of the atavistic memory of a beautiful girl claiming to be a salamander.

And I got carried away by that stream of thoughts swimming faster. In the other world, the crouched afternoon brought with it the laziness of the sun, shade, and humidity from the moss as it advanced languidly and romped above and below the refuge. The wind's spell and the reflecting water came into different worlds, coinciding in a single dream. In this dimension, the already-almost salamander perceived herself as a woman in the curious look of a *cá* when she came out of the water. However, while she lived inside the pond breathing through her gills, she vaguely remembered a fish that wanted to jump out of the dam in concentric circles. And she continued to lean on her four legs as she thought of a *cá* swimming awfully close to the sky, inside a pond located between two worlds. The young salamander is dress in black and yellow.

Tilden Park, September 1969

*U*nder the shadow of the sequoias, the afternoon would continue (advancing) immensely, setting minute by minute from the birds' constant chirping. There was something imaginary (suggestive) in the smell of eucalyptus, the rumbling freshwater, silt, dry leaves, a silence of tiny noises, and eternal sleep. Because on the other side of poetry, there would be Thanatos waiting patiently. And Eros would find himself behind this very reality waiting, angry, even though the afternoon continued to advance, bursting with new realities, exploding, coming into being, and falling on the other side of the Imagination.

Cristina Salaman would also experience that very afternoon falling immense, languid, and sleepy behind her sleeping eyelids. Defeated by the tranquility and peace that emanated from the place, she dreamed of becoming a salamander. «The illusion of reality is in the showcase of dreams —thought Cristina—; the perception of reality in its reflection —she confessed to herself as she entered that quantum region of dreams.» At 6ix in the afternoon, Cristina fell soundly asleep.

September 18, 1969

It was the last day we had news of them. Someone remembers seeing them navigate the intersection of Bancroft and Telegraph streets in the city of Berkeley. She, dressed in black corduroy trousers, a blouse, and yellow sandals. He, in black sandals, grey trousers, and a white shirt. Nine days later, as far as could be inferred, the media learned that Cristina Salaman was a loner (24 years old) and a little fond of social gatherings. She was also imaginative and fully inclined to her studies and beautiful. She had a boyfriend, Christian (25 years old), as lonely and withdrawn. They were both vegetarians and did not smoke tobacco. They did not drink liquor or take drugs either, but they loved to love each other in the open field and under that tree. They seemed to have no vices, but, after a "joint," they discussed The Teachings of Don Juan by the Peruvian Carlos Castañeda, a book that practically all the young of that time read. It was the youth of the sixties who questioned the established Reality. Cristina and Christian were esoteric ecologists and epicureans. He studied film in the graduate program of the San Francisco Art Institute. She studied Biological Sciences in the graduate program at the University of California (UC), Berkeley.

The city of Berkeley

Christian Fisher and Cristina Salaman met accidentally in Tilden Park in the early Spring of 1969. Both (each on their own) had given themselves the task of looking for a place (particular) where they could freely breathe peace and serenity. Perhaps, a site located in the unfolding of a contiguous dimension. Or in some region of dreams or, maybe, on the other side of the Imagination. On April 4, 1969, their lives crossed in this same refuge, lost in the dimensions of memory. Here, they talked about their positions on experiencing Reality as mere instants of consciousness in this very spot. Christian's argument is about the image's transformation, which seems to place the cinematographic Reality in the marker ego's dichotomy with the imaginary you of the masses, and vice versa. Cristina defended the adaptation that individual organisms undergo when suddenly their environment is changed. Police corroborated by the relics found: a chemistry notebook and a 16 mm film camera. Both objects, left next to a pond surrounded by litter. However, the truth is that no one knew what happened to Christian Fisher and Cristina Salaman on September 18, 1969. After a while, the TV news declared them missing.

In the mirage of the dream

In the area adjacent to the pond, at the foot of the redwoods, under the leaves. The ants argued enthusiastically: « Life plays in the mirror of reality, that is, the metamorphosis of time.»

Saigon, September 18, 1969

In a remote spot in the woods in Vietnam, a pond surrounded by leaves witnessed the terrified scream of a *cá* filmmaker: A dam surrounded by napalm! —This is not Tilden Park! — The salamander replied.

Bach-Tuyet Tran saw herself walking through a forest of sequoias in the dream, where the path led her to a pond surrounded by leaves. There she came across a 16-mm film camera and a chemistry notebook. She was tired and decided to lie at the feet of a young sequoia. «The film of

the 16mm camera coincides with the script in the chemistry notebook»,
thought Bach-Tuyet Tran before the dream defeated her.

Tilden Park, September 18, 1969

Cristina and Christian fell asleep at the foot of a sequoia after
smoking a joint and making love. They dreamed of a pond guarded by
a salamander. And with a *cá* trying to get out of the water. Curiously, she
was the salamander, and Christian was the fish; their anguish became
a nightmare as they both heard each other shouting: «this is not Tilden
Park!»

Massachusetts Institute of Technology

«The account would remain in the ontological reunion of a
dream. Reality is the relative topography of the conjugation of the
corresponding time of the verb crossing a quantum declination», assures
Eliza Weizenbaum in cyberspace. It is worth noting that Eliza was
a chronicler in non-real-time. Coincidentally, in real-time, a young
woman named Melissa Dykes wrote her hypertext fiction for the
Interactive Fiction Writing Course offered by Dr. Murray at Harvard
University's Department of Literature.

UC Berkeley, September 18, 1999

Approximately 30 years away (the same space corresponded to
the same time), a student of literature, dressed in black sandals, gray
trousers, and a white shirt, asked: «What happened on September 18,
1969?». The 24-year-old, dressed in black corduroy trousers, a blouse,
and yellow sandals, replied: «the age of the salamander came with no
traces of real-time.» And both continued reading the end of the poem
titled *La vista, el tacto,* by Octavio Paz.

In the MIT Media Lab

It would be 6ix in the afternoon on September 18, 1999, when Melissa Dykes finished her hypertext fiction titled, *The Dreampond*.

At the same time, at UC Berkeley

Juventino Buenrostro continued writing on his Dell PC: «it would have been 6ix in the afternoon on September 18, 1969, when the gaze of a salamander captured the shade of the refuge». Juventino stopped typing, took a sip of coffee, and reread the paragraph he had just written once more. At that moment, he stopped and argued with himself: «the conjecture of the present may well also be the memory of the future. Would it be possible for the present to be eternal?... The present is a bubble of time within another bubble of time, which floats in the void. Of course! —He told himself—, the dimensions also go within their bubbles, connected to filaments that become entangled with each other». And he went back to writing on his Dell PC.

Here (you and me), in this Reality

Reader! Your expression of disbelief says it all. Let me give you an example by way of metaphor to try to explain this phenomenon to you. Imagine an isosceles triangle standing like a pyramid, with the uneven side resting on the horizon. In this isosceles triangulation, the event «September 18, 1999» occupies one of the triangle's lower vertices. And, at the other lower vertex, «September 18, 1969». All right, you take the third vertices. However, you are the only witness to the simultaneity of both events. Not them! As they are at horizon level. Believe me! The same thing is happening in both refuges at the same time. Since one is the reflection of the other in another dimension. Just like you and me when you are reading about me. That is, we are in the same space and at the same time, and; at the same time, not in the same area and; the same time.

OUTER SPACE: THE SCREEN DARKENS

At 6ix in the afternoon

An ethereal voice hears commenting —an imaginary being finds himself in the square root of his negative space-time. It is known, by some, that the square root of a negative number is called imaginary, that is, the square root of minus 1ne:

$$x = \sqrt[2]{-1}$$

—The Imagination of the mind —a voice is heard to say.
— Of whose? —You interrupted, a little confused.
— Yours! —Clarified the ethereal voice.
— Mine? — You inquired in doubt.

The everyday normal-visible Reality, within the micro- Reality, within the macro-Reality, you heard a voice, within your mind, that in metaphoric form told you:

—Like Russian dolls (Matryoshkas), one inside the other, inside the other.

— {REALITY [Reality (reality)]} —you recited mockingly.
— Which one? —I asked you.
—The one that you conceive —your inner voice challenged you.

We both stared into the eyes of this page; then we closed the program to shut down the PC; the Dell computer screen went from light to dark; that is, from 1ne to zero. However, the refuge continued to exist somewhere in cyberspace. Because, according to Octavio Paz, «Light is time thinking about itself.»

Somewhere in the brain

—*En la duda de la verdad, ¿qué es la realidad?* —Mind asked.
—*La perspicuidad del Tiempo* —the image answers.
—*Nada es real sin evidencia* —you said.
—*Nada es real sin un observador* —I replied.

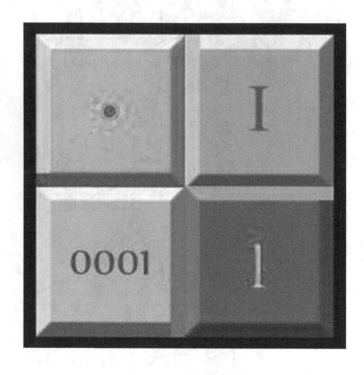

1NE **w̃** IN PART **w**

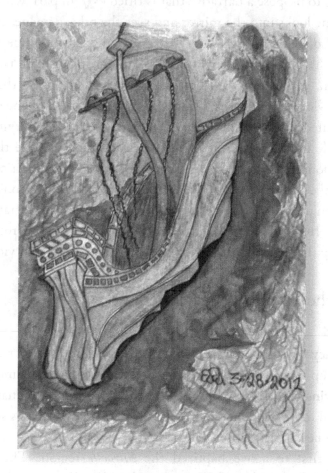

Narrative
©1999 Edel Romay

A REFERENTIAL NOTE

*C*ome! I invite you to reflect on the other side of the mirror. Don't doubt it. Today is an elusive space of time. Today is an elusive time of space. No, I'm not kidding you. Believe me! Today outlines a tomorrow and a yesterday playing hide-and-seek because a collage of memories is chasing us. No, I'm not kidding you. When the Ñ looks at the mirror, it looks like a W. And when the W looks at the mirror, it seems like an Ñ. The union of both becomes a single letter. Come, I am going to propose a narrative that is titled « **w̃** in part W.» In other words, one looks into the mirror and sees the other's image, the other who is also seeing himself, who is also formulating the same question that you have already asked yourself before: which of the two is the projection, you or me? And I'm getting to the conclusion that 1ne is zero and vice versa. That is, you are at that point where time seems to be measured in binary numbers. That me, in that you, trying to be intelligible in the spacetime or in the time-space. You are the verb's conjunction of the verb "to be," whereas I am the conjunction of the tense of the verb *ser* or *estar*. I am *conjugación* and *tú eres* conjugation. *Yo soy* conjugation. And you are *conjugación*. See! The narrative goes like this: 1ne looks into the mirror and sees the other mirror's image mirroring the same manifestation until it reaches zero, and vice versa.

In the house of the other being[2]

*T*hey were so many and so linguistically different that reality was knotted up like a symbolic skein in the archaeology of memory. You, no knowing it, had cut the thread of the historical continuation and then tried to reweave the skein again. What a mess! And, as such, you needed a new logic to interpret the signs.

The first to arrive baptized the *Suroeste* region. The second, Southwest. And neither of them cared what this place was called before

---

[2] Martin Heidegger (1889- 1976) "Language is the house of the true being."

they came. Okay! The English language arrived a century after Spain established the Spanish language. Then, two European languages began to dance on the landscape of what is now called the United States of America. Also, I want you to interpret this narrative as a quantum holism because the *Suroeste* is the Southwest and vice versa. THE REALITY of Reality depends on the language you rely on: *Español* or English, or a third language. The author, dreaming, dreamt that he dreamt dreaming that he recreates himself as a reader who also reads himself daydreaming as an author, and vice versa. The reality, in both cases, is almost the same, a slumber; that is, awake dreaming awake.

{The REALITY [of a Reality (of a reality)]}

The clock kept track of time in the bedroom, and the hands continued to turn in front of the Roman numerals, which undauntedly watched them. The almanac, immutable, continued to mark the weeks; the scattered remnants of a narrative waited for the author to be incarnated on the desk. And you are already reading it! And I hardly intended to write it. Don't doubt it. On the other side of this reality, there is another Reality and, within it, another one. And in each of them, two languages coexist, one devouring the other and vice versa. Perhaps, like a mirage within a mirage. I'm afraid you haven't seen the "Matryoshka" Russian dolls from your reaction of surprise. One inside the other, inside the other, inside the other.

In the space of one second

He woke up or thought he woke up. «What a recurring dilemma! Both realities are so similar that it's challenging for me to distinguish one from the other. I had gone to bed with the faithful purpose of finishing "today" what I had started "yesterday." Inevitably, Today will be yesterday. Today is ephemeral. Today, inevitably, was becoming an accumulative "yesterday." The truth is that we function in the past. A moment ago, you were reading the title and, and a cosmic nanosecond ago (160,000 years), the human conjured up time, time conjured up the verb, and language trapped time in the declension of the verb; space where the I is projected in you and vice versa». In that lucubration, he suddenly saw himself advancing towards the study without any difficulty and moved from one place to another just by thinking about it. He had a 360° vision, which allowed him a broader perspective. He heard a voice vibrating in the void that told him: «In the dream, time is not present, nor past, nor future; it is the void that invents itself as the past of a future present.» And he perceived himself without a body.

It just so happened.

In the bedroom, the clock struck 8:00 a.m. and the calendar, in silence, marked Wednesday, July 9, 1997. All this exists perhaps because you are reading it and imagining it. Do you understand me? The narrative is embodied on a blank page only because you continue to write it on the desk. In other words, the first word is written in the present past, since I am reading it, and as you read it, it will become the current memory. In other words, the eternity of the present fluctuates between two singular gaps.

At that very instant

I woke up! Or I thought I woke up. «Dejà vú,» I thought and made sure I had a body. I was happy to see myself naked, taking up a place in space; however, I had the feeling that something or someone was always watching me. I heard noises as I left the room and went to the studio to rummage through my writing. The title jumped out at me: «Part of the Imagination,» and as I read it, I felt like I was sinking into a river of letters, a sea of words, a gale of images...

One week ago *(Una semana antes)*

«Part of the Imagination» was born after reading 2wo books consecutively for 5ive days. I was looking for answers to the many questions I have: What is the nature of imagination, how does the brain create the Mind, where does the creative ring lie?

30 years ago *(1969, Berkeley)*

What I'm about to tell you happened 29 years ago. It may seem implausible, but it is not as inexplicable as it seems, even though the reality of dreams is, for the moment, difficult to quantify. Nevertheless, dreams happen in the Human Mind, and, as such, they must have a logical explanation since almost all humans participate in that Reality of Dreams. And it is precisely on that reality that I am going to lean, a reality as real as this reality in which you and I participate.

The curious thing about my dreams is that they followed one another consecutively. That is, I woke up, and the next night they continued. And all this happened during the summer of 1969 in the city of Berkeley. I lived a couple of blocks from the university in a small studio apartment at 2333 Channing Way. There, for 17 nights, I dreamt of an interactive episode: I was at Kip's, a restaurant bar on Durant Ave., between Telegraph Ave. and Dana St., having a beer when, suddenly, two hippies appeared in front of my table, demanding *spare words*.

—*What!* —I exclaimed—, you must mean *spare change*.
—No —they insisted—, we want to talk to you.
—And, what about? —I asked.
—*About Literature!* —they answered vehemently.
—Why about literature? —I enquired, a little confused.
—Because you have brought us here —they immediately challenged me.

—Me! And how did I do that, may I ask? —I raised my voice in an irritated tone.

—In your dreams —they answered in unison.

«What strange guys—I thought—, I›d better humor them. They seem to have come from another time. However, that smell of patchouli is classic of hippies. They›re probably «stoned." Colombian marijuana, no doubt—I thought to myself.» I smiled a friendly smile. I wasn't going to contradict them.

—What are your names? —I asked politely.
—*Yo me llamo Miguel, jovencito, y tengo cuarenta años.*
—And you?
—My name is William, and I am twenty-three years old.

At that precise moment, I realized that they each spoke their language; one, *Castellano*, and the other one, English. Interestingly, the clothing and both languages reminded me, I don't know why, of the year 1587. And the most entertaining thing was that I understood them entirely when they spoke. They settled down at the table, and we began to chat excitedly. William, the more restless one, was flirting with the two waitresses who served us. And I was forced to inform him:

—The blonde one is called Christina and is from here; the other, the brunette, is called Nora and is Russian.
—From here? —asked William.
—Yes, from the United States of America —I told him.
—We discovered America —intervened Miguel.

We agreed to continue seeing each other in the dream because this dream did not end when I woke up but resumed the following night. And so on, until we reached the count of 17 teen nights. We met at Kip's; the next three nights, at Larry Blakes, a restaurant bar on Telegraph Ave., between Durant Ave. and Channing Way. And the last seven nights at The Albatros Pub, at 1822 San Pablo Ave. By the way, they always initiated the conversation, so they told me that we had met before «in the Old World» on one of those occasions. They emphasized «Old World» with a specific sardonic tone. Besides, I initiated this meeting due to my interest in the literary work of both. So, it was me who have transported them to my present reality. The truth is, listening to them tell their stories was fascinating.

On one of those nights when Miguel left with Nora, William confessed that from 1585 to 1592, he traveled through Spain and the Mediterranean. He visited Italy, Greece, Turkey, and North Africa. «Travelling illustrates," he said in a complicit tone. But seven years were too few to savor the cultural diversity with which I interacted. However, the trip allowed me to explore the universal drama of the human condition more closely. As you well know, between 1589 and 1613, I wrote my best tragedies: *Hamlet, King Lear, Othello, Macbeth...*».

Finally, William managed to become Christine's lover and Miguel, Nora's. And I was left with neither of them despite my Machiavellian efforts to take them away from those two. In the end, I had to swallow my jealousy. These letter unicorns had magic in their words. And there was nothing I could do to conquer those women again. Miguel and William had won. However, we talked a lot about literature. Strangely enough, they spoke in their language and understood each other wonderfully, and I spoke to each of them in their speech, and the three of us understood each other perfectly. It is striking that William accused me of being tragic and Miguel of being a dreamer. And I thought I was a romantic. I never saw Christina and Nora again. I never forgave them for choosing them over me.

{TIME [of a Time (of a time)]}

*T*ime is the most prominent event in our mortal universe, yet we do not have the remotest idea of how it came about. Without time, however, a narrative would be meaningless. So, my encounter with

Cervantes and Shakespeare in the city of Berkeley is not my story; it happened in deferred quantum time. Miguel told me something about the coincidence of time that made me think. And his narrative went like this:

—When William was born, I (Miguel de Cervantes Saavedra) was 16 years, seven months, and three days old (approximately). And I died one day before him, in 1616, at the age of 68 years, six months, and 22 days (around). William died one day before his birthday. We both died in April and the same year, 1616.

—What a coincidence! —I exclaimed.
—*Don't be fooled* —intersected William—*Miguel loves the esoteric.*
—Just like you, *my dear William* —answered Miguel sarcastically.

In retrospect, nothing is real without evidence

I want to share, briefly, two of my last readings, which, without doubt, left me with deep impressions, and with this, perhaps, you can understand my dilemma of locating the reality of time in the reality of the dream. Besides, I read both of them in Shakespeare's language, in (modern) English. The first book is a collection of articles that pose various perspectives on science. The second book deals with what we know and does not know about the Mind. If time allows, take a look at them; I found both fascinating: Nature's Imagination: The Frontiers of Scientific Vision[3] and The Creative Loop: How the Brain Makes a Mind[4].

(In parentheses), the past indefinite

Miguel, taking advantage of the fact that William had gone to talk to Christine, reminded me that his most significant literary production period was between 1590 and 1613.

---

[3] John Cornwell, Oxford: Oxford University Press, 1995.

[4] Erich Harth, Massachusetts: Addison-Wesley Publishing Company, 1993.

—Mostly, I wrote a series of short novels slowly. Although the one everyone knows me for is *Don Quixote de la Mancha*. I wrote so much. But it was poetry that gave me the most headaches.

Miguel was silent as William approached the table. He was with Christine bringing us more beer and a large pizza. Christine looked more beautiful than ever; however, William never quite got the hang of her temper and made fun of my jealousy. I felt an uncontrollable urge to wring his neck at times like this, but I held back and chose to smile like an idiot.

Albany, CA (1999)

From 1969 onwards, Cervantes and Shakespeare's language intertwined in my Mind, forming unique images, each of the autonomous and independent, and when interwoven, they mixed ideas that enhanced each other. I am a master of both languages, as one might be a master of two mountain fillies. And I didn't want to lose my Spanish accent in my English just because I didn't feel like it. I hope you don't mind my whim. But let's go to the first book.

—Nature's Imagination: The frontiers of scientific vision — *interjected William.*
—*La imaginación de la naturaleza: las fronteras de la visión científica* —Miguel pointed out.

I stared at them without saying a word, but they didn't even flinch. And you, please forgive this interruption; Miguel and William are like that. They come and go in my Mind without asking permission to do so. You'll get used to it along the way.

Now I'll explain to you how the first book came into my hands. And let me tell you, reality is congruent with the dimension in which you move. I left home without a plan, only driven by the idea of walking. When I realized I was walking into Barnes & Noble bookstore, which was just a few blocks from my house. Once inside, I wandered among the shelves looking for nothing specific. That's what I was doing when I met John Cornwell, who offered me Nature's Imagination. I took the book and headed to the cafeteria. I leafed through it several times until Roger Penrose had caught my attention.

—Must Mathematical Physics be reductionist? —inquired John Cornwell.
—*¿Debe ser reduccionista la física matemática?* —insisted Miguel.
—I don't know — I said flatly —. *I don't know.*

—The article raises the concept of holism as mathematics —Miguel assured me—, which led me to speculate on the idea of reductionism.

—Obviously, the behavior of the whole (of the things we study) is governed by the action of the parts that make it up. There is no doubt about that —Cervantes assured me— but.

—What does holism mean? —inquired William.
—One moment, let's break it down.
—There you have an impossible triangle! Do you see it? —said, William.
—I said, let's break it down!

*T*he beauty of the impossible triangle is display before my inquisitive gaze. There is no doubt that the dimensionality it presents leads to a constant geometrical change in our minds. I observed it, and indeed the question arose: where does the impossibility lie, due to what particular property is the triangle impossible? I turned my face to where they were and stared at them as if looking for an answer; yet, impassive, they remained silent. I chose to shrug my shoulders and be quiet as well. And I turned my face towards the impossible triangle. The beauty of this triangle is unique. Come, come closer, observe it with me. Let's try to locate the impossibility in a specific corner of the triangle. We could perceive that the triangle belongs to the third dimension (3 D).

—*Wait for a second! Let's talk about it like we know* —exclaimed William.

—Thanks to the perspective, we can interpret 3 D from 2 D — Miguel explained.

I see now —I told them that we are located in the 2 D constructing the 3 D in our Mind on this page. —I asked enthusiastically—. Once we were in 3D, we could say that the impossibility had disappeared. Impossibility is not found in the rest of the triangle. By hiding or removing any of its corners, the impossible triangle suddenly becomes possible in 3D. However, when we study the structure as a whole, then the impossibility reappears.

I kept silent for a few seconds while I watched to see whether they were listening to me. They cocked their heads as if to tell me to continue my explanation.

—Let us visually imagine that we cut the impossible triangle into three pieces as illustrated in the second figure and then assemble it in its original form. In this way, we could continue to cut it, and each piece would allow the triangle to manifest in 3D; the «process» of reassembling it is the «operation» that makes it impossible again.

—Cohomology —said, William.
— Impossible triangle cut and reassembled —Miguel agreed.

—In mathematical terms, it goes like this —I said—: you take all the pieces with all the «reassembly operations» and, factoring in the «process,» we arrive at what is called cohomology. In other words, the measure of the impossibility of the triangle, in this particular example, «the degree of impossibility,» could be assigned with a single actual number. Therefore, cohomology is a concept that is perfectly well defined in holism as mathematics.

Proceeding with the same reasoning, let's move on to explore something about the knot: where does the knottiness reside in the knot? At first glance, it seems simple. However, explaining «knots» is more complicated than defining cohomology. The scientific investigation of the knot's inherent quality in the knot dates back to the early 20th century. Today, it is a whole science. Like the impossibility of the impossible triangle, the knottiness cannot be located either. It is a property of the structure as a whole.

Another example would be the Möbius strip. We could ask: where is the twistiness? Let's see; if we take a strip of paper, twist it once, and then glue the ends together, we will have built a Möbius strip. Then, wherever we cut it, the twistiness would disappear. The twistiness is a characteristic of the structure as a whole and cannot be located at a defined point.

Once again, mathematics offers a series of theories from the study of twisted structures called knotted fibers. We can conclude that holism is a respectable concept within modern mathematics. Today, with quantum mechanics, physics has become holistic in more ways than one.

Nothing is real without evidence

Are you still with me? Are you still reading? Forgive me for taking you from one dimension to another with my exaggerated concern about REALITY, about reality. But you have proven it; it is not enough to see, perceive, look, imagine.

Take what I'm about to tell you as a metaphor. On one of my several trips to Lima (Peru), two tiny ants slipped into my portfolio, which I always carry by hand. And so, among my notebooks, they traveled with me to South America. Once in Trujillo, a city north of Lima, I left them outside. I saw them wandering around the desk, and then I knew nothing more of them. However, comparing the tiny ants' size with the distance from Berkeley (California) to Lima (Peru) and then to Trujillo made me think about the dimension of space and time, and vice versa. Their tiny reality is affected by the reality of the flight between two geographical points on the globe. The reality of that evidence was located in my brain. But I wonder: How? *¿Cómo?*

(In parentheses), the brain creates the Mind

—The Creative Loop, how does the brain Make a Mind? —stated William.

—*El anillo creativo, cómo crea el cerebro a la mente* —said Miguel.

—Our distinguished researcher Erich Harth, author of Windows on the Mind, in the physics of perception, offers us a persuasive theory that attempts to explain in detail how the brain creates the conscious individual, that «I» that we all experience as separate from the outside world of things. Inquisitively, it proposes, first, how this organ creates its world of images and how that same world compares the real world of objects and events. Second, what role time and space play in the image world; that is, in the world of the Mind.

At that moment and in unison, Miguel and William asked:

—Is there anything else we can say about consciousness? What is sensation? What is intentionality? What is creativity?

—Harth takes us out of the old Newtonian world of machine models in the brain and launches us into the almost mystical field of contemporary physics. I dare to call it true scientific poetry without my daring to minimize in any way the scientific rigor that has been given to science. On the other hand, Stephen Kosslyn, from Harvard

University, states that «thinking is the ability to contemplate something in its absence.» Similarly, we could say that creativity is the ability to contemplate something that has not existed before. For example, the philosopher Daniel Dennett speaks of multiple sketches of a scene observed by homunculi hordes (tiny little men), each expert in a different area of knowledge. All the variables of perception, indeed, all variety of thought or mental activity, are achieved in the brain by parallel and multiple interpretation processes and elaboration of sensory inputs. For example, look at Dennett's design with me. Okay, two scenarios, but you are aware of one at a time —I said—. What we can perceive in the design are two faces in profile looking at each other or glass, but, on closer inspection, we realize that the two interpretations never coexist. Instead, your perception changes from one to the other indefinitely. In other words, and this is a personal position, we find ourselves with two realities separated by two separate dimensions.

—What do you mean? —inquired William.
—I don't understand —added Miguel.

The imagination

George Berkeley's[5] motto was «To be perceived,» which made me focus on reality, Reality, Reality. By the way, I don't know how true it is; it may or may not have happened at all. The important thing is that it makes you think.

They say that someone approached Picasso after seeing Demoiselles d'Avignon and queried why he didn't paint people the way they looked. To which Picasso replied:

—What do people really look like?
Then the person took out a photograph from his wallet and added:

---

[5]   George Berkeley (1685-1753). Irish philosopher, ordained Anglican priest who use to say: *Esse est percipi.*

—Just like my wife looks here.

Picasso looked at the picture, gave it back to him, and said:

—She's very small, don't you think? And she's flat, too.

We usually realize how much our brain has to add to the image to represent a recognizably real scene, Erich Harth[6] assured me as we talked when I read it. For example, the work of American painter Mark Tansey, *The Innocent Eye Test*. At first glance, you can see a cow, to which some gentlemen (on the left) are showing a life-size painting of cows. A couple of scientists are standing with notebooks on the right, ready to record the animal's reaction. There is none. The cow may well be looking into the void or thinking about a beautiful pasture field.

The Innocent Eye Test, by Mark Tansey, is hung in The Metropolitan Museum of Art, New York. It is monochromatic. With the sepia colors of the old photographs standing out, —Erich verifies me—And this emphasizes that the real cow, to which the painting is being shown, is itself a painting. As flat and lifeless as the other cows—. Although all cows have been painted the same size and style, we insist on seeing one cow as genuine and the others as not. The first cow seems unimpressed. And why would she be? Cows have no idea what a painting or a picture is.

The geometry of sleep is flat

Flat as in 2-D, that's Mark Tansey's painting. So are the pages of this book you're reading. However, when you intervene, you create other dimensions, other realities. That is what William and Miguel assure me.

(In parentheses), Wednesday, July 9, 1999

He woke up or thought he woke up. He made sure he was wide awake. He did little gymnastics. He took a glass of water and very

---

6   Erich Harth, (1993). *The Creative loop: How the Brain makes a Mind.* Massachusetts: Addison- Wesley Publishing Company.

carefully looked at the mirror. He looked back at himself and thought he saw only emptiness. But as he rubbed his palms on his face, he saw the manuscript on the desk and his other self-reading the last page, and that made him doubt who was who in that unfolding of himself. Fortunately, Miguel's question, «Which one are you referring to?» made him answer immediately:

—I don't know. The reality is that I do not distinguish between the author and the reader; when I think I am the author, I happen to be the reader. When one arrives, the other disappears, and vice versa.

— They appear and disappear simultaneously — I think I heard Miguel say when a riiiinnnng pulled me out of «that reality.»

The alarm went off at 8:00 a.m. sharp

Finally, I woke up, the almanac next to the clock categorically insisted on the date: Wednesday, July 9, 1999. In the bedroom, the light of the summer morning had pierced the window, splitting the penumbra in two. And I was left to contemplate the parallelogram of light that surprised countless floating dust particles. The reflection of the light on the mirror drew a voice that said:

— Without time, the concept of «history» has no meaning in the narrative. And I was left meditating in my sleep.

Wednesday, July 9, 1999

At the last riiiiiiinnng, he finally woke up. The clock struck 8:03 a.m.; he reached for his slippers, went into the kitchen to get his usual glass of water, and looked for his notes on the dining room table. And there, on loose sheets of paper filled with notes, was what he had written.

USA *(The Southwest),* the Southwest, a pause

Guided by Cervantes and Shakespeare's fountain pen, the language manifested itself amidst the desert, the cactus, the rattlesnakes, the pavement, and the skyscrapers, ignoring a myriad of magical and dreamlike images dancing in the echo of more than 500 other languages. The human mosaic of the *Southwest* is only perceived as interacting between the past and the future because a dream is a stage where one builds and rebuilds. Because I dream that we write, paint, invent, create. Because «Part of the imagination» is a metaphor for *español* and English.

{REALITY [of a Reality (of a reality)]}

The clock kept keeping track of time. The calendar supposedly continued to announce the same date. On the desk, the sheets of paper were listing a narrative that could well be the geometric skein of a quantum weave; however, you only saw the letter Ñ flying in the company of the letter W, going towards the horizon. You turned the page without thinking about it, and you were left looking into the void. And in that emptiness, you kept a meditative silence; you had stopped reading what you were writing..., you were completely awake.

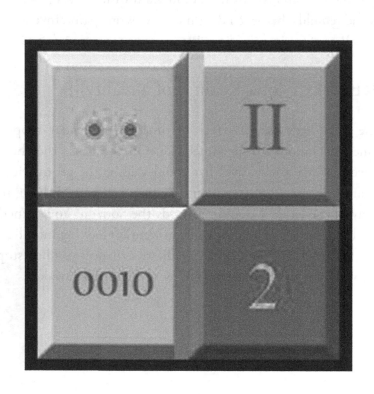

THE IMAGE

Narrative
© 2000 Edel Romay

INITIAL REFLECTIONS

Eros arrived from heaven wrapped in a purple mantle.
—Safo[7]

Dialogical note

The blonde boy saw a blonde girl in the dresser mirror.
The *Chimu* boy saw a blond boy in the closet mirror.

The fickle light

—The light of darkness sees the darkness of the light —said the elf.
—The existence of the first justifies the presence of the second —answered the witch.
—Mirrors in the darkness are blind —said the elf.
—Mirrors in the light are reflective —answered the witch.

In the bedroom

Equidistant to his geometries, when Pat, in New York, looked at the dresser mirror, he exclaimed to himself, «Patricia!»; when Anselmo, in Huaranchal[8], looked at the dresser mirror, he shouted to himself, «I am blond!».

---

[7]   [1] Powell, Jim (1993). The Poems & Fragments of Sappho. (p. 10). First published in 1993 by Farmer, Straus and
Groux: The Moonday Press.

[8]   The town of Huaranchal is located in the province of Otuzco, in the department of La Libertad, Peru.

IN THE UNITED STATES

*I*n New York, where skyscrapers made their nest in America, the mind and idea reflected the structure's exterior glass. In the reflection of the imagination, elves, and witches from the other world «depicting tales» the diversity of an immigrant family's reality. And it happened that, in apartment number 1492, in the half-light of the bedroom, the mirror of the chest of drawers reflected a ray of light, coming from the window facing east, an angle α on the face of a child. In that instant, the child was inventing a look that immerses in the mirror of memory. And behind that image, every morning, a girl would discover stories of an androgynous adventure. The years passed, and the mirror grew in person. Then, the adult mirror lived, died, and resurrected between «she» and «he.» In other words, «he mirror» reflected itself in « she mirror.» And when this happened, «she mirror» reflected in the Spanish language. Then, « he mirror,» within the mirage of «she mirror,» became the transvestic imagination

The quantum memory of reflection: the simultaneity of the mirror

A beautiful Anglo-Saxon bruja witch drew the Greek letters [fi] Φ and [psi] Ψ, and claimed that Φ was Pat and Ψ was Anselm. With a gesture of complicity, the elf that was with the Anglo-Saxon beautiful witch added:

—In the quantum imagination, there is the tendency, the approximation, the potentiality that the statements about the propositions (Φ) and (Ψ), when reflected on the same dresser mirror, project their respective desired magical silhouettes.

—Look! —replied the witch—, the binary style of narrative masterfully incorporated into the connected form *ni-ni* of the Spanish (neither-nor of the English). I will symbolically call this form $((\Phi \downarrow \Psi)$, which translates into «neither is Pat a woman nor is Anselmo blonde.»

In that instant, the spell was cast, the same light would be reflected simultaneously at two different points in the American Continent.

(In parentheses), memory

*C*amille's best friend in Spain was a transvestic schoolmate called Patricia Naranjo. At the age of 17, during the summer of 1919, Pat Naranjo decided on his conviction to be *Patricio Naranjo* for the entire world.

Patricio possessed a unique subtlety for politics, an innate inclination for poetry, and a masterful music fluidity. As an activist, he claimed that one had to visualize feminism to transform the ideas of female submission that society so malevolently instilled in women. On the other hand, as a poet, she initiated Camille to the poetry of Sappho, a Greek poetess who was born on the island of Lesbos. He familiarized her with Aphrodite and invented lyrics to describe the beauty of Sappho. And like Sappho, Pat also possessed an enigmatic beauty, «green moon black,» like a gypsy painted by Lorca[93]. With black, curly, short hair and an olive complexion, his features framed a pair of expressive eyes of the night gazing «green, how I want you green.» And he had a voice like a nightingale when he sang *Cante* Jondo poems.

Patricio had a unique attraction to the cafés of yesteryear. Madrid, for example, was losing its oldest and most traditional cafés replaced by new and luxurious ones, which lacked that warm bohemian atmosphere. The new taverns didn't have that old and cozy scene either.

---

9 [3] Federico García Lorca (1898- 1936). He was a Spanish poet, play-wright and theatre director.

Throughout the city, one could sense this new transfiguration. A transformation that, over the next 9ine years, the two of them would inevitably experience.

The two of them began to make history and legend. In one of those bohemian dawns, Patricio, just like that, introduced Lorca to Camille. And, from then on, they spent time and sang and laughed together. Patricio recited verses of Lorca and his inspiration in cafés and taverns. The years began to speed by like wild horses, full of poetry, art, and singing. By 1928, Lorca left for his homeland leaving Camille and Patricio feeling sad, none of them knowing they would never see each other again.

On December 28, 1929, a decade fell upon her. When she woke up, Camille was alone and, at the same time, accompanied by a note from Patricio resting on the pillow next to hers:

"Camille: Oh, how hard it is for me to love you as I do! So long... Pat».

For Camille, the world dropped in a tear that was greater «than the big salty sea (*que la mar salá*).» Spain. Her Spain. The Spain she would never see again had gone away with him for good. And with her.

The Fiction of Fantasy

*P*atrick Ingarden Claudel heard from his mother, in Spanish, absolutely everything. Camille's narrative was an oasis where the fantasy of reality is subtly mixed with the truth of fiction and vice versa. Through her mother, Pat acquired Spanish and learned to speak it, a language he would identify with the metamorphosis of reality, poetry, and theatre.

Camille's magic-oneiric fantasy knew no bounds. Pat learned from her mother how to disguise fantasies with bodies of reality. From childhood, He/She knew her mother's inclination towards her. As a child, Patrick began by disguising himself as Patricia. Eventually, he would start acting like Patricia. The two played a monologue that, in time, would demand real space for the language of dialogue. Camille was the mirror for this virtual image of Patricia to become a reality. Patrick grew up in Patricia, and Patricia grew up in Patrick. During her teenage years, the character gradually acquired an independent life and became a flesh-and-blood woman.

Pat claimed to have a sister named Pat. Pat, in English, rationalized it as mirroring seduction. In English, Pat's name was comfortably ambivalent about gender. The ambivalence that Pat knew how to use intelligently.

At 44, Patrick Pat Ingarden Claudel was a linguistics professor at the University of California, Berkeley. At 27, he had earned a Ph.D. from Harvard University and had lived in Berkeley for 17 years. He spoke several languages, including Spanish, almost as a native speaker. Because of his facility with Polish and Russian, one could argue, without a doubt, that his linguistic heritage came from his paternal grandparents. The same could be said of French and German concerning his maternal grandparents. However, that sweet, almost atavistic taste for Spanish and everything Spanish was due solely to Camille's mother.

The theatre of poetry

Camille Claudel Bultmann lived and was primarily educated in Spain. By the age of 17, she had easily convinced her parents to study Spain's cosmic cultural labyrinth. Thanks to her wise decision, she enjoyed intensely experiencing the Spanish avant-garde poetry, better known as the Generation of 27.

Camille studied Philosophy and Arts at *Universidad Complutense de Madrid*. And she met *Federico García Lorca* in person, already, at that time, considered the most original of the newest poets. And a Madrid in a state of entropy.

Camille was thin-bodied. Physically, at first glance, she looked very much like the German actress Marlene Dietrich. Added to this, of course, after the first impression, was Camille's unmistakable face. A face with very well-defined complex features, where the highlights were those blue eyes, cold like the North Sea. Fleshy lips and an eagle's gaze. Blond hair, straight, short, and stylish, with a left parting. Camille knew how to balance her erotic and provocative beauty with a rhythm of austerity and distance. She knew how to impose herself with character in any situation with a strong temperament, no matter how challenging.

Her stay in Spain had become complicated, so, at the age of 27, in the spring of 1930, when she visited her parents as she did every year, Camille finally decided that returning home would do her good, and she stayed in Paris. In the Paris of Montmartre and Montparnasse. In the Paris du Nord-Sud, a newspaper founded by the poet Pierre Reverdy, named after the metro route, connects two artistic areas: Montmartre to the north and Montparnasse. Today, this route is known as No. 12. Nord-Sud would become one of the essential avant-garde newspapers during the war years. Meanwhile, for Camille, Nord-Sud would become the compass that would mark her deepest artistic emotions in the following nine years.

After a few days of being in Paris, she learned of the surrealist movement's crisis and the verbal quarrel between Breton and Magritte. After 27 days of being in Paris, in the Café de la Place Blanche, she met Edmund Ingarden, a chemical engineer. Edmund was tall, slim, with long thin hands, and big green eyes. Blond, with curly hair and exceedingly feminine features. Although there was nothing artistic about him, he was fascinated by Camille's surrealistic world. After seven months of courtship, they were married. As a wedding gift, Patricio gave

Camille a Greek amphora, along with a card in English that said, «Do you remember Sappho? Like her, I melted with love for you, once and long ago, Pat». Camille read, in Spanish, the contents of the note several times in silence: «*¿Te acuerdas de Safo? Como ella, me derretía de amor por tí, una vez, hace mucho tiempo…*». And she cried her eyes out. And she smiled as she recalled Pat's statement that to enjoy life to the full is to know how to reach love, poetry. After all, the dimension of the body does not end where the skin begins.

Mirage in transition

*A*t the end of September 1932, the first male child was born, which Edmundo insisted on calling Vladimir, the name his maternal grandfather had in life. Two years after Vladimir, André was born. And in André's third year, Antoine was born. However, between life and death, space of spaces, Camille and Spain suffered the Civil War. Meanwhile, Camille, impotent, was bathing in a sea of tears, first for the murder of Lorca in 1936 and second for Patricio's death in 1937. Fascist Spain is bathed in a sea of blood. Both Lorca and Patricio were accused of the only crime that was different from the established. 1939 also brought a premonition of the Second World War, a suspicion that rapidly penetrated «everyone's dream» like «razor blades.»

Edmund's nightmare was somewhat relieved at the end of November 1939, when he received good news from his relative in America. The Ingarden family emigrated to the United States in mid-December of that year. Camille was once again three months pregnant. Patrick was born on June 27, 1940, six months after his family settled in New York. Camille had already been wanting a girl since André. Her hope was dashed when the doctor at Mount Sinai Hospital, with all the tact in the world, informed them that, after this birth, she could not have any more children. So, Patrick would practically become the daughter she had so longed for.

In New York, Camille began to experience the bohemian city of the 1940s, just as Lorca had experienced New York City in the early 1930s. She frequented Spanish Harlem and dedicated her life, body, and soul to avant-garde theatre. The American Press often misunderstood Camille's theater and, by the 1950s, was full of controversy. Camille's last play, Transvestite Mirror Seduction, a script written for theater, film, and television, was unfortunately never heard of again: she died in a car accident when Pat was 17. After his mother's death, Patrick created the reality of his sister Patricia in another city. And without thinking twice, he underwent reconstructive cosmetic surgery to get a pair of beautiful women's breasts. This way, he would more fully enjoy the androgynous love that he loved so much. Pat would never set foot in New York again.

In the quantum memory of reflection

*I*n Huaranchal, South America, there in the mountains, where the clouds made their nest, the mind and the idea seemed to be reflected on a water eye. In the reflection of the imagination, Chimu and Moche witches «depicting tales» the story of an indigenous family's diversity. And it all began that morning, when sitting at the foot of the bed, he contemplated the emptiness of a wardrobe mirror. Memory was a witness to memory. That morning, the window let in a beam of light at an angle α and landed at the image that the wardrobe mirror projected. Then the miracle materialized. The light from the blond Christ painting bounced off and transformed the picture. The image the wardrobe mirror projected of him became a blond face. Anselmo's face and nobody else's. A look he kept in his imagination. And there he played and would play as if it were true.

In a region of Chimu memory, indigenous sorcerers established two statements on the Andes' back: Φ and Ψ. They claimed that Φ was Pat and Ψ was Anselmo. And when Φ reflected himself, he saw a beautiful blonde woman. And when Ψ glanced at himself, he saw a blond man. In other words, the image reflected the multiple illusion of the reality of a child making up a face behind the mirror in the closet. And so, the years passed, and the mirror became a man. The child-adult lived, died, and rose every day, reflecting the exact image of the blond child. However, in the dream, the waters of the *Rimac* floated, pronouncing names in Quechua, and although the mirror immersed in the dream insisted on reflecting a blond man, the other mirror, the one that looked at itself, reflected the image of a Quechua man disguised as the sun.

«The plane of the mirror is analogous to the process of reasoning used in dialectics —said the Quechua sorcerers—. The mirror's plane compares a thesis (object) with its antithesis (ima1ge in the mirror). The plane of the mirror, in its absence, shows us just that: reflection is a way of dividing and synthesizing ideas. Removing "the plane of the mirror" is an act of synthesis; the antithesis disappears within the thesis.» In that instant, the spell had been cast; the same light would be reflected simultaneously in two different points of the American Continent.

(In parentheses), memory

Anselmo Avalos del Campo grew up with the firm idea that he was indeed as blond as the Christ who lived in the reflection of the wardrobe mirror. Later he would pretend to be blond like the Christ in the painting in his room in Lima. Or, perhaps, blond like the English capitalist. Or blond as a German actor. Maybe, as a Hollywood hero, who, apparently, knows everything when he is acting, something like feeling very clever. In the future, he would act like those heroes who give the exotic impression of someone who has just arrived from a created adventure. «Acting out a fantasy is like being a movie actor,» he said to himself. He'd be coming from here, or there, or beyond. He was coming from far away, from infinity. Coming, perhaps, like that blond doctor who had come to the neighborhood when he was a child. The doctor's face was so similar to the Christ in the picture that Anselmo assumed that, like Christ, that doctor cured everything or almost everything. He, in particular, could not be cured of that indigenous skin he was wearing or that certain highlander way of talking. Although he cried several times to medic Christ: «Doctor, please make me blond.»

When he turned five years old, they emigrated from Huaranchal to Lima's city at Aunt Juana's invitation. Simultaneously, in 1956, while they were settling in the Rimac, Elvis Presley became a millionaire in the United States. When he turned 7even, his mother was employed as a maid in the house of a gringo doctor. At the same time, Fidel Castro, that same year of 1958, proclaimed «Cuba libre» to the four winds.

Lima, Peru

Doctor Christopher Shappiro lived in San Isidro in a vast, two-story, white-walled house, and the colossal library smelled of camphor. The courtyard garden was full of flowers. And the red roof shone, challenging the wind.

Mrs. Shappiro was very beautiful. She looked very much like Marilyn Monroe and spoke on the phone all the time. Everyone in the house was blond, except his mother, the chauffeur, the nanny, and the dog. The dog was a massive Doberman as black as night. The only white thing that glowed was his four sinister fangs. However, the dog was looking after Christ, who suffered from epileptic fits. Mrs. Eva Shappiro said that the dog barked an hour before the girl had her attack as if to warn her. A warning that everyone took very seriously. Christ already knew and lay on the floor on her own. Perhaps that is why Mrs. Shappiro took such great care of the dog.

Christine and Christopher's junior were six-year-old twins. Christopher Jr. didn't have epileptic fits. They were so similar that it was tough to tell them apart. Anselmo, in particular, liked Christ very much. Although they moved to San Isidro at the doctor's house, his mother kept the little room in the Rimac district. That room was all they owned. His father, Sergeant Avalos, had abandoned them economically. So, as a point of reference, that room would represent the axis of memory. That would be where their nightmares, games, and ghosts would be. Now the sergeant, their father, would go looking for them from time to time. And, his mother thought that it fitted that she should keep cordial contact with him. So, she would have to adapt to a new routine on Sundays at Rimac. The other 6ix days to San Isidro, where in the morning, very early after breakfast in the kitchen, the driver would take them to school. The twins to Roosevelt College and him to the public school.

He liked to read and hear the news a lot. What he read most were newspapers and magazines. Mrs. Shappiro was the first to know about his love of reading. And of the marked preference she had for Christ. And, in turn, Christ loved it when Anselmo read her the comic and social pages. Every afternoon he was allowed to stay in the library and read. On Saturdays, he played with the twins in the courtyard. That's how the years went by until he graduated from elementary school with great success and good grades. And, much to his regret, he had to leave the doctor's house. Age was betraying him. It had become evident that Christ liked to talk to him too much. And since Mrs. Shappiro was uncomfortable with this situation, she spoke with Anselmo's mother and proposed a solution. Anselmo would have to leave the house, but they would not abandon him. The Shappiro family would pay for him to go to school, and they did so religiously until he finished secondary school.

A pause (in parentheses)

*T*he Rimac room became his new universe, so that by 1968, at the age of 17, he was graduating from high school, at the same time that he received the news that his mother was leaving for the United States with the Shappiro family. Coincidentally, that same year in Mexico, in Mexico City, a history marked the Tlatelolco Massacre in *Plaza de las Tres Culturas*.

By the beginning of 1970, he started studying at *Universidad Garcilaso de la Vega*, beginning the famous Agrarian Reform of *General Juan Velasco Alvarado*. In early 1971, he left for Santiago de Chile due to the adventurous insistence and goodwill of a little blonde USA citizen (*gringa*) who, by the way, paid everything in dollars. Thanks to this good Samaritan, he had found the philosopher's stone. He would never work for anyone. He would never work for the capitalist system. He would never pay taxes of any kind. He would act to his ladies the anti-capitalist per se. All he hoped for was blessed change. For that reason, he would call these little Samaritan *gringuitas* progressives from then on. And he would go to bed with them with the complete and most fervent illusion that, by making love to them, alchemy would somehow do him the favor of turning him into a blond, like the lord in the painting in the Rimac room. Unfortunately, every morning, the mirror would shout the same song, «*Cholo soy y no me compadezcas* (Half-breed I am and don't pity me).»

He arrived in Chile at the height of Allende's socialist government. He came amid the Chilean transformation. A transformation that, without a doubt, would also transform him into something. Taking advantage of the occasion, he amicably left the gringuita to get together with a pretty progressive Chilean girl and, of course, blonde. Over time, this woman helped him financially, shamelessly giving him money. She connected him to the literary world and, using her influence, enrolled him in the Catholic Church. He left the Chilean girl for another gringa, who, in time, provided him with another exciting adventure. In fact, by the end of 1972, he and the gringa of the moment somehow perceived the danger. And just in time and rightly so, they set off for Lima, Peru. When they left Lima for Los Angeles, California, Allende's government suffered a fatal *coup d'état*.

The permanent erratic residence

*A*nselmo Avalos del Campo was indeed a mystery. Little is known about him. And of the very little, if one wanted to discern, one did so by inference. He said he was 33 years old and identified himself as a journalist. He boasted of having interviewed significant figures of Latin American literature, including Neruda himself. He claimed to have studied at the *Universidad Garcilaso de la Vega* in Lima, Peru. Anselmo also bragged about having a master's degree in sociology from *Universidad Católica de Santiago de Chile*. He said he had a mansion in the *Rímac* and a more oversized bedroom than a library; the bedroom had more books than a library. Anselmo also said that he had two children with two different women. And he boasted that his father was, or had been, a general of the Peruvian army decorated three times. Whatever it was, the reality was that Anselmo lived in the San Francisco Bay Area. And there was a distinct possibility that he had previously resided in Los Angeles, California. However, it seemed that he had been living with some stability in the city of Oakland lately. He was a native of Peru, a detail he did not emphasize too much. And when he is forced to comment on it, he did so with biblical parables. Among Peruvians, this was of little use to him since his countrymen soon realized the truth. That is why he is rarely seen surrounded by Peruvians. But he did prefer the company of Chileans to the point that, sometimes by mistake and sometimes by association, people would mistake him for a Chilean. He spoke only one language: Spanish. And his English was not very good. Also, he was editor-in-chief of a local, non-profit newspaper called *Transición*, which was sustained by the ad sales he promoted and which, in return, paid for his wretched existence. He was always short of money, even though he boasted of drinking fine, expensive wines. Besides this and other contradictions, it seemed that he did not understand his situation. He maintained total anonymity for the International Revenue Service (IRS), for the value-added tax (VAT), since he had no known employment. His Social Security number seemed to be another mystery.

Anselmo Avalos del Campo had also cultivated that image of permanent erratic residence and love relationships, by the way. Perhaps, his behavior is because, at all times, he wanted to give that exotic impression of someone who had just arrived from a magical adventure. Illusion disguised as mystery and fantasy. For example, one day, he could be coming from here, as the next, he could be arriving from there. One day he could be with one blonde girl, and the next with another, and another, and so on—unusual behavior for someone who, on the other hand, claimed to be the opposite. But even more insubstantial was his melodramatic performance when he replied: «Well-to-do guys (pituco) are inconsistent about the reality of appearance. I am the alternative. We must remember that not everything that is perceived is necessarily part of the same reality. I, for example, give love without asking for anything or almost nothing in return. I am a lover of progressive love». Anselmo claimed that this was true. He said that the song *No soy de aquí ni soy de allá* described him thoroughly: «As if someone had written it for him.» At one point, when he discovered that the audience was questioning him with their eyes, he joked, «As if all of that were true (*A como si fuese cierto*).» «Anselmo seems to live in a reality that is out of place and time,» many of his friends thought. «He›s like the Rimac, talkative, but unlike the Rimac, he lacks direction,» thought many others. Many ignored him. Others openly doubted him.

The City of Berkeley

*T*he virtual image of a desire could be called a mirage because, mostly, «you see what you want to see.» However, on that Friday night, July 13, 1984, the mirage would take on authentic, unforgettable tones. For both of them, that night of the 13th, their lives' esoteric aspect would become the axis of reflection, the apparent source of crystalline waters. They would unknowingly cross the apex between «reality and the mirage.» Congruent with both realities, each would project that desired reality into the eye of the mirror. The mirage, then, would run parallel to the parallel mirage of multiple realities. Finally, the inner mirage that both separately desired would become the other parallel reality. That is, the actual reality, projected on a virtual mirror, projecting the desired reality.

On Friday night, July 13, 1984, the Bar & Grill at the Shattuck Hotel was packed with people, mostly foreigners, more than any other night. Due, perhaps to the proximity of the University of California. And the mixture of foreignness and sophistication that the city of Berkeley experienced. Whatever it was, the noise was intense, and the atmosphere projected familiarity and many physical contacts that night. Pat had been frequenting the Shattuck Hotel's Bar & Grill since 1982.

On the contrary, for Anselmo, that night of Friday the 13th was his first time. It would have been 9:00 p.m. when Anselmo, slipping like a fish through the crowd, got to the tavern. Once there, he had to fight his way through to the bar. Meanwhile, the two bartenders on duty could barely cope with customers' and waitresses' requests on the other side of the bar. At the bar, Anselmo repeatedly insisted in English: «*Beck's please...*». Until that moment, he was unaware that Pat had been following him with her eyes from the first moment he stepped into the lobby of the Shattuck Hotel. So it was that already at the bar, Pat let Anselmo get acquainted with the atmosphere. He watched him for quite a while before deciding to approach him. Finally, he waited for the right moment when the bartender brought him Beck's beer. Meanwhile, oblivious to what was soon to come, Anselmo took a crumpled five-dollar bill out of his pocket and handed it to the bartender. Pat took the opportunity to intervene:

—John, one Courvoisier and add his becks to my tab —and turning to Anselmo added—: (¡*Permíteme invitarte*! *Tu presencia me hace recordar a un viejo amigo de lima*) Let me buy you a drink! You remind me of an old friend in Lima.

Anselmo was stunned, dumbfounded, not knowing what to say. First, because of the ease with which this gringo spoke Spanish and the speed, he approached him so elegantly. Second, because of the unexpected nature of the situation. «How does this gringo know that I am Peruvian,» he asked himself, looking for a solution. Meanwhile, seeing that he was not reacting, Pat placed his left hand on Anselmo's right forearm and asked again: May I...?

To which Anselmo accepted with no resistance:

—Thank you. What's your name?
—Patrick Ingarden Claudel... And yours?
—Anselmo Avalos del Campo.
—Come —said Pat—, let's go to my table.

Anselmo found two little gringuitas who spoke Spanish at the table, half a bottle of wine (1976 Mayacamas Cabernet Sauvignon), and several sandwiches. «The gringuitas are devilishly beautiful; one of them especially so,» Anselmo thought to himself. As for Patrick, he frowned: «He seems to be a bit of a prick but a good gringo». Because for him being good people was a sign of being a prick. He looked at the three characters, with that crouching look that he used to opt for on occasions like this one, and, little by little, he adopted, according to him, that sophisticated and playful attitude of a progressive lover from an exotic world. In his fantasy refuge, Anselmo almost always resorted to the «quixotic guerrilla» abandoned on «an impossible mission,» looking for his «Dulcinea» in the mountains of his most conflicting emotions. And then, he becomes an actor in a drama where he is the star character.

For Anselmo, that night was a night of conquest. «What a feast at hand!» he thought. And he ate everything and asked for more. And he drank everything and asked for more. And with his average English, he chose to display, what the English would call, a colonial charm; that is, a colonial spell, seen from Britain. He had the girls gawking at him. His pseudo-intellectual gestures (of course, he invented) are intended to describe Latin America and those committed to the revolution. He spoke of imperialism, how the bourgeois, and the capitalist, the minority, share the world's wealth. Then he said of love, of that love that Neruda speaks of. He talked of poetry and social commitment. And that he, in particular, hated bourgeois love and its oppressive morality.

«The bourgeois is a male chauvinist! (*machista*!)» he stressed vehemently. That's why he believed in free love and the total liberation of women. And he added that all this could be achieved in a classless society. In the end, Cynthia gave him her phone number and, of course, they made a date to go to dinner. In the euphoria of the moment, he felt like a well-to-do (*pituco Don Juan*) and asked for another bottle of red wine. «But what a mess I just got myself into — thought Anselmo — penniless and inviting to dinner. What am I going to do now? I, who live in a tiny little shack in a poor neighborhood in the city of Oakland». And he began to talk to himself: «Don't panic... That's it! I'll have to go to my friend the cook, the one who works at The Reef restaurant. Of course! *Fernando*, my Mexican friend. After all, I've done it before. *Fernando* will cook one of those dinners he usually cooks. In exchange for what? Well, in exchange for the expected promise. We'll have to get him a little gringuita just like the Chyntia».

Patrick could see that Anselmo had no money and this thing about him being a journalist. Well, we'd have to see. What was clear, however, was his charm, that uncompromising grace that inspired confidence and abandonment. A very particular contradiction of the Latin hustler —Pat thought. That is, of the marginalized Latino. That charm and instinct of feline survival, on the one hand, and lack of manners and worldly sophistication, on the other. «Perhaps that's where success lies with the occasional American woman —Pat meditated—. Seeing guys like Anselmo in action is fascinating. For example, to witness the display of strategies used and reused to capture Chyntia's admiration is exhilarating. Keeping her interested in the conversation and getting her to agree to give him a ride home was extraordinary». With equal charm, even though he had spent the entire night asking for food and drink, somehow, when it came to paying, he made no effort to settle the bill. However, Pat was not bothered by this. That night of the 13th was a night of mirrored reflections for Pat: a night where seduction began to present itself as a living, self-reflecting mirage. For Anselmo, that night of the 13th was a night of unprecedented desire. That is, in a way, for both of them, it was a night where sensual pleasure became erotic and promised to become poetry the following day. However, Pat proposed, in a very well-orchestrated way, an invitation to dinner the following Friday at his house. The reason was the arrival of her sister. —My sister, Patricia, arrives from Spain. So next Friday there's a dinner party. —And he proceeded to take a picture from his wallet—. See, she looks just like Marilyn Monroe.

(In parentheses), memories

*A*nselmo, that morning, already in his room, in the company of his solitude and fantasies, dreamed of the *Rimac* room. The image became clear to him; he once again experienced that mirage of the blond Christ on the reflection of his face. Anselmo imagined himself to be blond like the Christ doctor. And he saw himself making love to Mrs. Eva Shappiro while she, with her skirt, pulled up to her waist, was talking on the phone in the kitchen. Transported, in another dimension of the same dream, Christ, with a crown of gardenias and with his blond hair fallen to his waist, at fifteen years old, was signaling for him to go into the river. Once in the water, Christ possessed him with caresses of liquid fish while the black Doberman barked. There he sensed Marilyn Monroe's tender gaze like lightning. Because in the Rimac room, Marilyn Monroe was his lover. They were both socialists. In another corner of the dream, he was blond and gallantly riding along the banks of the *Rimac* on a white horse. On the waters of the Rimac, his face was reflected like a yellow sun. Suddenly, he was transported to the mountains, where Pat, voluptuously naked, made loving gestures to him while the yellow sun and the green wind kissed her all over. Tall, blonde, enigmatic, Pat undressed him by caressing him with wet petals of pink tulips. Meanwhile, early in the morning, «Brown of the green light moon (*morena de verde luna*)» falling in profile from the heights.

The enticing seduction of the long-awaited dinner

Anselmo arrived via public transport at 8:15 p.m. at Patrick's. Patrick lived in a Mediterranean-style house near the intersection of Marin Street and Euclid Avenue in the city of Berkeley. He rang the doorbell twice. And when he was about to ring the bell a third time, the door opened softly to make way for a tall, elegant, and gorgeous blonde woman. The red dress with its suggestive décolleté and tightness fell to her ankles. And her narrow feet were wearing red triple-banded, high-heeled sandals. All this and her womanly scent made Anselmo open his mouth and stand still for a moment. Unable to articulate a word, he said to himself, «She does look like the Marilyn Monroe!» And he closed his eyes as if to catch such a delightful image. He opened them when he heard:

—You must be Anselmo — Patricia modulated the sentence with a very horny tone.

—Yes —he replied—, Patrick invited me to dinner. —And accepting the challenge, upon himself, of seducing this blonde girl, he entered the house displaying a certain air of importance.

In the living room, comfortably installed, under the influence of the warmth of the fire emanating from the chimney, while pouring him a glass of Cuvée Don Perignon champagne, Vintage 1978, Patricia explained to Anselmo —Her brother had called her to do the cooking that will take a few minutes—. In the way Patricia said it, her voice flowed with flirtation in the air, which produced an indescribable horniness in Anselmo. —Patrick apologized for not getting here on time for dinner —continued the beautiful wench —there was an unforeseen event at work that required his undivided attention. So, she will take care of him by Patrick's particular recommendation. Patricia also warned Anselmo that she was nowhere nearly as good as her brother in the kitchen. But there is no need to be alarm. Next, she recited the menu in English and Spanish:

- !978, Mayacamas Chardonnay.
- Barbecued prawn and seafood with mango and clavelline sauce.
- Spinach soup and garlic bread.
- 1976 Mayacamas Cabernet Sauvignon.
- Salt & pepper prime rib with mixed vegetables.
- Apple-pecan crumb pie; Brandy Torres; coffee or Tea.

Anselmo had learned about by the second glass of champagne —in an easy conversation—Patricia's exceptional taste for music, literature, art, and the contagious sentimentality of Andalusia. And in passing, she also told him about the admiration she felt for Federico García Lorca. Patricia confessed to him, in secret, that Federico was like her soul mate. She let him know that her mother had been a Federico friend while she was studying in Spain. In detail, she talked about her mother's adventures when she was a student at Madrid University. On one occasion, while drinking wine in one of those taverns, Federico, very seriously, told her: «If you ever have a daughter, call her Patricia.» Perhaps for this reason or another, her mother had bought her an old house in Granada with gardens where the aroma of lemon, olives, and orange blossoms mixed.

By the third glass of champagne, Anselmo's fantasy of conquering this beautiful lady inebriated his reason. Patricia's sensuality turned him, as if by miracle, into a poet and a seducer. Under the sign of Sagittarius, the night vibrated intensely. At the same time, seductively elusive, in the comings and goings of the kitchen to the dining room, Pat displaced a marked flintiness by singing *Cante Jondo* poems, accelerating Anselmo's desire to trap her in his arms. And without a second thought, Anselmo came up behind her and held her breasts with one hand and her belly with the other while kissing her on the cheek. From the skin of both came a taste of almond, sugar, and sunshine. Meanwhile, delicious sparks of fire and pleasure sprang from the fireplace. Pat's centaur body became voluptuously soothed and caressed as it touched him with a rhythmic movement of her behind. Pat turned slowly and kissed Anselmo's lips eagerly. The kiss was an oasis, forest, and sea. Beach, wind, and rock. Desert, sun, and horizon. In short, depth of desire and aroma of moss. Dewy humidity and the taste of tulip in April. Water and wind. Sun with a taste of sand. Then, Pat gently withdrew from Anselmo, revealing an intoxicating beauty with glowing eyes and burning cheeks. Anselmo took the opportunity to caress her all over, whispering a string of beautiful words in her ear. Pat, kissing her neck, replied:

—The heart alone can be taunted.

Anselmo, in response, kissed her forehead, the tip of her nose, and her lips. And crossing their glasses, they both drank every last drop of champagne.

—Chablis is the best wine for seafood —Patricia apologized, extending two glasses and the 1978 Mayacamas Chardonnay—, but I love this one —. And she decided to let him sit at the head of the table while she sat to his left.

Flowered shrimps in the shape of a clitoris, mussels, oysters, and bulbous oysters, bathed in saliva and wine, danced Dionysian dances from their mouths. Kisses and caresses played a morbid, rhythmic, and provocative wait. The wine ran out, and they uncorked another bottle. Then the aphrodisiac language took its course —a course in marine flavors and aromas. Taste and smell became a symphony of clicks and erotic noises. Their burning eyes exchanged multiple appetites. While their lips full of desire became messengers of caresses, attacking all the senses.

Then it was time for the soup, and with the spinach soup and garlic bread, the long-awaited 1976 Mayacamas Cabernet Sauvignon wine. Like themselves, the succulent lamb chops were in the deliciously long wait, being handled and nibbled on first and then sucked to the bone. The kisses with fat, pepper, and wine were like alternating currents. Lust, sensuality, and appetite produced conjugated suns and tidal waves. Between sips of the Mayacamas, all this and more was spread in an *allegro passionato* in the body of silence. The stereo (The Firebird) played Stravinsky's music, diffusing over their naked bodies' surface. And so, it was that the following day, their desires became fantasy and the metaphor an explosion of mutual involvement, as Anselmo finally woke up blond, and Patrick woke up rightfully as Patricia.

FINAL REFLECTION

> Eros, the limb loosener, shakes me again
> —that sweet, bitter, impossible creature.
>
> —Safo[10]

Dialogical note

The American saw a beautiful blonde woman in the dresser mirror. The Peruvian saw a handsome blond man in the closet mirror.

The fickle light

—The light of darkness sees the darkness of the light —said the elf.
—The existence of the first justifies the existence of the second — answered the witch.
—Mirrors in the darkness are blind —said the elf.
—Mirrors in the light are reflective —answered the witch.

In the bedroom

The image finally became true for both of them because, when Anselmo woke up, he saw a beautiful blonde by his side. «So, it was true,» he said to himself, as he gently approached her ear to whisper affectionately, «I love you, Patricia,» just as Pat opened her eyes and exclaimed, «Anselmo!»

---

[10] Powell, Jim (1993). The Poems & Fragments of Sappho. (p. 20). First published in 1993 by Farmer, Straus and Groux: The Moonday Press.

PERIPHERIES

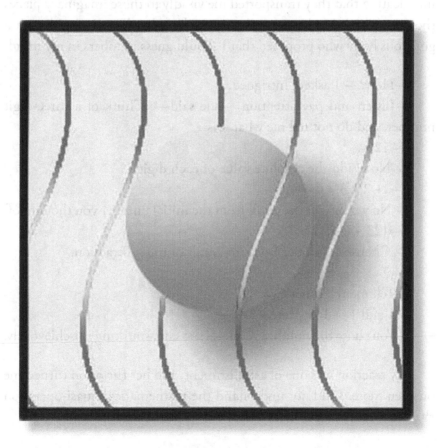

Narrativa
© 2000 Edel Romay

INTRODUCTORY NOTE

*T*his preamble could well be a presence of

An enunciation I learned in high school was called the Pythagorean triangle. Let me tell you how it happened. The esoteric thing here is that Eros and Pythagoras conversed in my mind. I still vividly remember going from my trigonometry text to my older cousins' naked women's magazines. And the erotic narratives I read there were so highly intoxicating that they transported me vividly to those imaginary places they described. I believe I still contemplate that beautiful girl with a gorgeous body who proposed that I should guess numbers in my mind.

—How? —I asked, intrigued.
—Listen and pay attention —she said—. Think of a three-digit number, and do not tell me what it is.
—«123».
— Now, add the absolute value of each digit.
—«1+ 2 + 3 = 6».
— Now, subtract the result from the initial number you thought of.
—«123 – 6 = 117».
— Choose a number from the result of the subtraction.
—«7».
—Tell me the other two.
—1 and 1 —I answered.
—You chose the number 7even — she said, smirking mischievously.

My reaction was one of astonishment, and her flirtation turned me on even more. I did not understand the mathematical quasi-operation that the beautiful girl had worked out in her head:

$$1 + 1 + x = 9$$
$$9 - 2 = 7$$

As I called her, we repeated it countless times and, Claraluz, as I called her, always guessed the number I had chosen. Imagination at that age is mind-boggling, so I chose to believe that the number nine was magical. Still, I later learned that if any number of three digits is deducting from the sum of its digits, the result is always a number divisible by 9. For example, let's subtract the sum of the absolute value of the digits of 876:

$$876 - (8 + 7 + 6) = 876 - 21 = 855$$

And the sum of the absolute value of the digits of 855 (8 + 5 + 5) is 18, and 18 is divisible by 9.

The same thing happened to me with the triangulation of the sphere. The demonstration was physically geometric. Two beautiful girls showed me that the ball I played football contains 12welve pentagons and 20wenty hexagons and that it is called a truncated icosahedron. Luz Aurora showed me this while holding my hand and playing with me. Then Alba Estela intervened to show me that the hexagon is split into 6ix equal triangles. And each pentagon is divided into five triangles. Then, the same operation is carried out for each triangle obtained, and each one is subdivided into four triangles. In other words, each hexagon is divided into 24-four triangles and each pentagon into 20wenty triangles. This process results in a structure called a geodesic sphere. Luz Aurora and Alba Estela took me by the hand and led me through what is known as the *Divine Triangle of Pythagoras*.

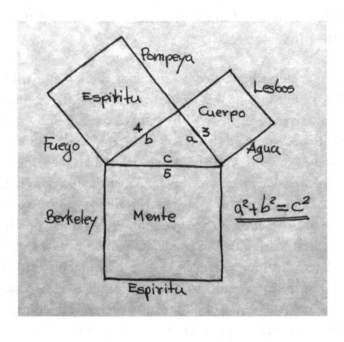

Vertex *A*

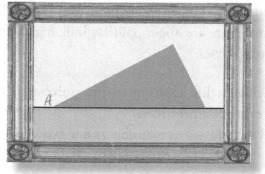

*I*t was mid-April, and the Campanile (bell clock marked 11:30 in the morning). Café Strada on the corner of College Ave. and Bancroft Way has crowded with students, and the bustle was intense on the terrace. Bancroft Way, too, was adorned with the agile legs of pretty girls in shorts that moved from place to place. The bustle of spring was contagious.

Do you hear them? They sound like a flock of little symphonic birds. See? Especially that couple there, in the background, in that corner. The one with the beard, who's listening to her, is bewitched. She is so gorgeous, who wouldn't be?

Of the two, she was the one that spoke most. All Eduardo seemed to do was follow her with very attentive eyes as she gestured while she talked. The fluency of her gestures made her even more beautiful. Her coquetry was innate.

—*Cogito ergo sum*— declared René Descartes in the void of images. But only Eduardo realized this, as at that very moment he began to talk to himself—: «I doubt, I think; therefore, I am. Maybe I have more questions than answers. I ask, I think; therefore, I doubt».

Eduardo was silently trying to articulate the conversation he had started with Deborah at Café Strada. Talking with Deborah had always been stimulating for him. And even more so on that day, after having made love like two cheerful sophomores. Although they were no longer sophomores, despite the youth, they exuded.

Deborah told him categorically that one of the many discoveries of 20th-century science was that the universe is expanding in all directions. And that the visible universe has a radius of about 14ourteen trillion light-years. And in that volume, there are about 350fifty billion giant galaxies and about 7even dwarf galaxies.

—The possibility of intelligent life existing in the universe is plausible— Deborah concludes, almost breathless.
—Plausible! —Exclaimed Eduardo— as plausible as our existence from out of the blue.

Deborah stared at him as Eduardo sipped coffee from a paper cup he held between his palms. Then, Eduardo and Deborah hold hands as if to justify the physical space they were enjoying. Both believed they heard, in that concise space of time, an ethereal voice that said:

—*I inhabit a world of probable selves, a world where present, past, and future incarnations of the human personality arise. The matter is only a local appearance of reference. Or, failing that, the possibility of acquiring a state of critical matter. In other words, the world exists not as a concrete reality but as waves of uncertain and intermittent possibility. On the other hand, the past, present, and future do not meet in a continuum at a subatomic level.*

They looked at each other intensely and tried to locate the voice they were hearing. All around Eduardo and Deborah, the surrounding conversations followed their ordinary course. They let go of one another's hands, each with their eyes fixed on the other as if wondering where those words came from. Deborah was the first to shake off her astonishment and ask:

—Did you hear what I heard?
—Yes! —Answered Eduardo.

But he had already lost himself in Deborah's blue eyes, which looked beyond his physical appearance. Under the table, perhaps as sensual support, Deborah caressed his thighs with bare feet. Eduardo's instinctive reaction was to grab her light feet with both hands, which, like fish, were trying to open his fly. «To tell the truth —he thought— talking with Deborah about cosmology is intoxicating.» Also, instinctively, and at the same time, Eduardo posed, in mathematical logic, the following formulation on a paper napkin: «(x) (x is a man . $\supset$. x is mortal)». And vocalizing, he expressed:

—No matter what x maybe, if x is a man, then x is mortal.

To which Deborah, translating simultaneously into Spanish, replied:

—*No importa lo que x sea, si x es un hombre, entonces x es mortal* —and she continued: There is no doubt that you manifest yourself physically as Eduardo, just as there is no doubt that I am your desire. I doubt I think; therefore, I exist. And this thing about being mortal could be questionable. The Eduardo from yesterday had a predisposition to undergo a metamorphosis. Today's Eduardo is eternal. Like the electron, the spirit seems to ignore time. Time is, perhaps, the changing state of space; however, the soul is the perfect form. The human being is perfectible. And the distance between them intercepts consciousness. And consciousness is the reflection of the mind, of the void. And the void is the whole. And the essence of the void is the perfect form. I ask, I think; therefore, I doubt —Deborah argued.

Angle α

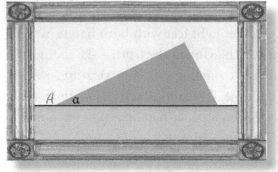

The sunny Saturday afternoon was lulled by music, incense, and works of art that were openly provocative to the senses. Arturo uncorked a bottle of Beringer 1993 red wine, cabernet sauvignon, Private Reserve and served two glasses, making sure to pour them just below the halfway mark. He picked up his glass, tilted it, looked at it, swirled it, looked at it again, smelled it, and finally took a sip.

—Ummm! —it's delicious.

In the studio workshop, Dianne's 27-inch by 36-inch photograph challenged the form, space. «And it is easy to perceive —Eduardo thought— that in addition to this erotic balance, there is evidence, so to speak, of Arturo's visceral and intuitive genius to make us accomplices to the multidimensionality that seems to exist between space and form. Arturo presents us with space as if it were the reflection of the form. Arturo has that unique ability to make obvious that which seems incomprehensible, as long as one chooses to use the seventh sense as a pilot». Eduardo found it fascinating that, along with blown-up photography, there was the 54-inch by 72-inch oil painting, inspired, of course, by Dianne's photography. Next to the oil painting, there was a poem inspired, obviously, by the picture. And next to the poem, there was the film script. Eduardo said to himself: «it is also worth adding that mystical relationship Arturo has with the number 9ine. For example:

"The sum of the absolute value of the digits of 27 (2 + 7) is 9.

"Likewise, the sum of the total value of the numbers of 36 (3 + 6) is 9.

»The product of 9 times 3 is 27.
»And the product of 9 times 4 is 36.
»Also, the sum of the absolute value of the digits of 54 (5 + 4) is 9.
»And the sum of the absolute value of the digits of 72 (7 + 2) is 9.
And these numbers —Eduardo paused for a moment— fit elegantly into the Pythagorean equation: $x^2 + y^2 = z^2$.

»In the oil painting, there are features of Aphrodite from the island of Lesbos. And satyrs from the island of Andros. Orchestrated in Pompeii, Eros manifests itself everywhere. On the other hand, the Southwest is host to nymph daughters of hippies intertwined with *Faunus* legal aliens. The sequences are charged with an impressionist realism, a surrealist reality, a fauvist conversation of 4our intimately intertwined natures. This painting needs to be interpreted with the sixth and seventh senses».

Arturo, in turn, had been watching all of Eduardo's almost imperceptible gestures. For Arturo, Dianne had always been the oasis of his inspiration. Because Dianne carried the dance of the electron in her blood. Because, somehow, Dianne made him an accomplice of that physical space that mixed with form and turned one into the reflection of the other, and vice versa. Ideas accompanied by images were integrated one by one in Arturo's mind, so much so that at that very instant, he once again heard Dianne's words: «You think, you doubt; therefore, you exist. Because you are my desire: ask, think; therefore, doubt». Arturo was in another world, but Eduardo's voice pulled him out of his trance:

— All the observable ordinary matter and energy of this universe represents 4.9% of all matter and energy produced by the Big Bang.

—Of course! —Arturo replied instinctively— 28.8% Dark Matter and 68.3% Dark Energy, as you scientists call them, are in the spirit —And he took two sips of red wine.

Eduardo strolled to the table where the glass of wine was waiting for him. And he performed the same ritual as Arturo before him: he tilted the glass, looked at the color of the wine, swirled the glass, looked into the glass again, barely put his nose into it, and took a slow sip of wine.

—Ummm! —He said—, indeed, it's delicious. —And then, looking Arturo in the eyes, asked him—: How were you able to capture so much beauty, harmony, and rhythm?

— All you see here is just 4.9%
—You're pulling my leg —exclaimed Eduardo.
—No, 95.1% is in the spirit —answered Arturo savoring the cabernet.

The mood set with a lusty rhythm of anticipation as the music continued to spread everywhere, along with Dianne and Deborah's laughter from the terrace.

—Let's see the girls —said Arturo.
—And this music, what's it called? —Asked Eduardo.
—*Trionfo di Afrodite* — Arturo stammered, squinting his eyes.

(In parenthesis)

*A*t the age of 18, Pythagoras lost his father. A death that affected him profoundly in the deepest depths. His uncle suggested that he go on a trip. He gave him some money, wrote him a letter of introduction, and sent him to visit none other than the philosopher Pherecydes on the nearby island of Lesbos. Pherecydes had thoroughly studied the Phoenicians' sacred book and instilled in Pythagoras the belief in immortality and reincarnation. Concepts that Pythagoras later took as the basis of his philosophy. The two became close friends, but Pythagoras did not stay in Lesbos for long. At the age of 20, he left for Miletus, where he met Thales.

A recurring dream had by all 4our

As in dreams, the vision of time is panoramic. Dianne, Deborah, Eduardo, and Arturo had the vivid awareness of repeatedly dreamt of the poetess Sappho and the poet Anacreon in those times and living in that reality! Dianne and Deborah saw themselves as being 18 years old. And Eduardo and Arturo, 27. Then, they saw themselves die at the ages of 63 and 72, respectively.

Echo of a voice inside the void

All right! Coincidence or not, this narrative takes shape at the precise moment you imagine it. Agreed! All this has its origin. Maybe it's the real fiction of an atavistic memory dancing in the dream. Or the peripheral reincarnation of the spirit.

Vertex *B*

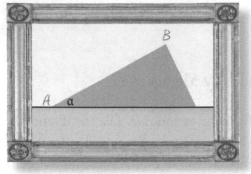

*D*eborah and Arturo lived on the hills of the city of Berkeley. Arturo fell in love first, and then it was Deborah's turn until they finally bought it. The house had that Mediterranean style that they so loved, and it sat at the intersection of Spruce Avenue and Acacia Street. It had a breathtaking panoramic view of San Francisco Bay.

Deborah was 27 years old, and Arturo was 36, and they had been together for nine years. Both were successful professionals and emotionally. Deborah had recently earned a doctorate in Nuclear Physics and was fascinated by cosmology. On the other hand, Arturo is inclined towards the arts, despite having a Ph.D. in Psychology. Coincidentally, both were graduates of the University of California at Berkeley.

*D*ianne and Eduardo lived on the Kensington hills. By the time she was 18, Dianne had inherited an enormous house from her parents at Arlington Avenue and San Antonio Street. Sadly, her parents died on a field trip to India when Dianne was about to turn 18. Fortunately, nine days after her parent's death, she met Eduardo, and they have lived together ever since. Oddly enough, Dianne was 27 and Eduardo 36, and they had been together for nine years. They, too, were successful professionals and emotionally together. Dianne had recently earned a doctorate in Comparative Literature, but she had always been fascinated by dance. Eduardo was a Doctor of Mathematics. By coincidence, they too were graduates of the University of California at Berkeley.

(In parenthesis), it is worth clarifying

These couples were little or not old-fashioned, dull; on the contrary, they were highly Epicurean. All 4our, in one way or another, had developed mainly at least the first seven senses. Perhaps they gladly celebrated the erotic part of existence; they used to contend with simple metaphors that nature celebrates the human anatomy in all its forms and dimensions. For example, «a persimmon can become a woman's beautiful derrière,» thought Arturo. Or, «A clam or mussel looks a lot like the flower of life,» insisted Eduardo. It is also worth admitting that, amid laughter, Deborah and Dianne claimed that a banana or a Geoduck Clam was eloquent without being less effusive.

90° angle

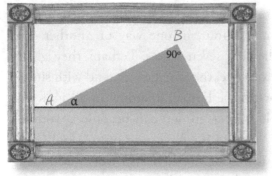

On the terrace, Deborah and Dianne were enjoying the sunny Saturday afternoon, the Beringer Cabernet Sauvignon Private Reserve, and the music of Carl Orff, which, like incense, floated dreamlike in the air. Both had a natural tan accentuated by their slightly fitted, off-white dresses with backs open down to the tailbone, revealing their monumental figures. At first glance, they physically resembled the film actress Demi Moore. Or oil paintings of nymphs from another era. Deborah wore it long and wavy with light brown hair, while Dianne wore it short and stylized. Unlike his partners, Arturo had light brown hair and was tall, muscular, and hairy. Eduardo was skinny, tall, blond, and also hairy. Arturo had short hair, while Eduardo's was long and straight. Both had stylized, well-groomed beards.

Deborah, sitting in a folding chair, stared intently at Dianne, closed her eyes, stretched her feet, and remembered again the dream where the experience was so clear that it was frightening. «It happened when the four of us were conversing with the young Pythagoras and the beautiful Sappho. At the same time, the jealous Anacreon recited erotic poems to Eduardo. Meanwhile, Arturo and Dianne, spellbound, tried to understand the Pythagorean triangle $3^2 + 4^2 = 5^2$. Curiously, Sappho caressed me like the sea breeze. This probably was one of the many reasonings that, at the beginning of the summer of 1976, crossed Arturo's imagination —thought Dianne, while caressing with her left foot Deborah's feet—. The Pythagorean triangle is enigmatic —she told herself and closed her eyes to capture better the dance of the numbers 18, 27, 36, 45, 54, 72, and 90—. Without a doubt, we were 18 and

27 when we lived on the island of Lesbos. And we are 27 and 36 now. And, of course, the dimensions of the photograph. But 27 and 36 also represent sudden death in Pompeii. The frescoes that Arturo painted of it in the Villa of Mysteries are still alive today in books. —Dianne breathed a deep sigh at the same time as she thought intensely about Arturo as she entered this state of slumber that, little by little, took her to another dimension where dates and known images arose one by one—. Indeed, in about 640 B.C. Thales of Miletus was born, and in 585 B.C., he predicted a historic solar eclipse. The great genius Thales and Egypt his poetry. The date of his death is not known. However, the appearance of Pythagoras in this fantastic setting of the period between 570 B.C. and 500 B.C. is worth mentioning. It was that in the year 552 B.C., they met and fostered a friendship of two years. Finally, Pythagoras left the island of Lesbos to meet Thales of Miletus. Pythagoras was a pupil of Thales when Thales was about 90 years old. Dianne opened her eyes when Deborah kissed her lips. Then they both fell into a sea of caresses. You and the sunny Saturday afternoon witnessed this. Because when Eduardo and Arturo arrived, the two women had already broken out in laughter.

The Albatross Pub (in parenthesis)

The 4our had met at the Berkeley Albatross Pub about 9ine years ago. And from the first time they met, they experienced the same odd feeling of having met before. But where? Coincidentally, the third time they met at the Albatross, a Hindu (Dianne's friend) revealed to them, in great detail, their 3hree clear and well-defined incarnations. These incarnations clarified the panorama. And a more intimate friendship began, precisely because the 4our shared the same experience. And the same dream.

Vertex C

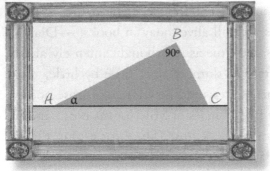

I am going to use certain well-established concepts to formulate my theory —said the Hindu master. In the duality of the human being, two universes unite and form a cosmic union. That is, every man carries a feminine charge within himself, and every woman carries a masculine charge within herself. The association of both integrates what is known as masculine or feminine. —And the Hindu master proceeded to draw the sketches that appear below:

MASCULINE

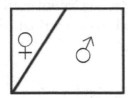

FEMININE

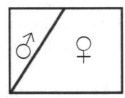

—On the other hand, it is worth remembering the definition of Cartesian coordinates —he continued to explain—. For example, a point can be located on the plane by its distance to two straight lines that intercept it, forming a right angle originating at 0. The two lines that intercept each other are called axes. One, the x-axis. The other, the y-axis. See?

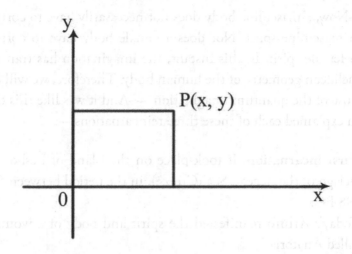

(In parenthesis), the metaphor

—I would like to propose the use of Cartesian coordinates as a quantum relationship of the spirit to the body —said the Hindu—. However, it should be noted that the body could become ♀ or ♂. In the same way that the spirit can become ♀ or ♂.

Look at the example:

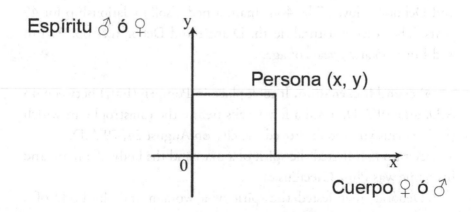

—Now, a masculine body does not necessarily have to correspond with a masculine spirit. Nor does a female body have to correspond with a female spirit. In this instant, the imagination has transcended the Euclidean geometry of the human body. Therefore, we will have to make use of the quantum imagination. —And it was like this that the Hindu explained each of these three reincarnations—:

"**First incarnation.** It took place on the island of Lesbos, in the archipelago of the Aegean Sea (Greece), in the period between 579 BC and 498 BC:

»Today's Arturo manifested the spirit and body of a woman and was called Anatoria.

»Today›s Deborah embodied a man's soul and a man's body and was called Siliano.

»Today›s Eduardo manifested a woman›s spirit and a woman›s body, and her name was Ciéis.

"Today's Dianne embodied a man's spirit and a man's body and was called Alcibíades.

»*The triangulation was* evident, despite the juxtaposition of gender. At that time, Arturo was Deborah's companion and, at the same time, Dianne's lover. On the other hand, Eduardo was Dianne's companion and Deborah's lover. The 4our maintained a solid relationship for 45 years. They died a natural death. Dianne and Deborah at 63. Arturo and Eduardo at 72 years of age.

»**Second incarnation.** It took place in Pompeii (Italy) between 43 A.D. and 79 A.D., until a few weeks before the catastrophe in which the Vesuvius volcano destroyed the city on August 24, 79 A.D.

»Arturo manifested the spirit of a man and the body of a man, and his name was Pliny Caecilius.

»Deborah manifested the spirit of a woman and the body of a woman, and her name was Postamia.

»Eduardo manifested the spirit of a man and the body of a man, and his name was Cornelius Tacitus.

»Dianne manifested the spirit of a woman and body of a woman, and her name was Lolia.

»The triangulation was evident, as evident as the Pompeii of those times was erotic. Even today, that eroticism has reached us via frescoes and statues. At the time, Arturo was Deborah's companion and Dianne's lover. Reflectively, Eduardo was Dianne's companion and Deborah's lover. It is not surprising that the patron saints of the city were Venus and Dionysus.

»The inhabitants of Pompeii were somehow aware of the meaning of living next to Vesuvius. Perhaps for that reason, they left us inscriptions and graffiti of the vivid belief that life must be lived intensely for as long as it lasts. And it is not surprising that these 4our Epicurean beings thoroughly enjoyed good sex, good food, and fine wine.

»Dianne and Deborah were born in Pompeii in A.D. 52. In contrast, Eduardo and Arturo were born in A.D. 43 in Rome. However, when they were nine years old, their respective parents were transferred to Pompeii. Deborah and Dianne were 18 years old when they met at one of those great feasts dedicated to Aphrodite. The same thing happened with Arturo and Eduardo. And so, the 4our, among the great excitement of wine, began their relationships, which lasted 9ine years. They lived in what is now known as the Villa of Mysteries. And it was there that they died suddenly in 79 A.D. The woman died at the age of 27. And the men, at 36».

The Hindu master kept silent for a moment, then he smiled and said:

—In this **third incarnation,** you represent the following:

«Arturo manifests the spirit of a woman and the body of a man (♀, ♂).
»Deborah manifests the spirit of a man and the body of a woman (♂, ♀).

»Eduardo embodies the spirit of a woman and the body of a man (♀, ♂).

»Dianne manifests the soul of a man and the body of a woman (♂, ♀).»

The four were silent, peering at each other expectantly while the Hindu read what they were thinking.

— Well, it's natural that you don't believe me, but I assure you that what I put to you is true ou yourselves have corroborated it in your dreams.

—In other words —said Eduardo—, we have transcended time and space in some way.

—But how? Interrupted Arturo.

Angle θ

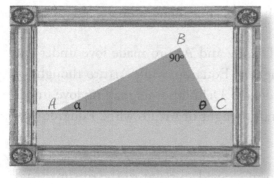

*J*ust as they enjoyed the Brahms symphonies or the sunset on a deserted beach, so they enjoyed their love affairs. For the 4our, these intense relationships were accepted without qualms, protected, and nourished. They were as natural as the rain or the sea, the wind or a hug. It just happened. The delivery was complete. The balance was fixed. The truth, perhaps, lay in the cosmological geometry of the city of Berkeley. That is to say, the truth of reality as the reality of truth was expanding in all directions. And the horizon of this expansion seemed to be represented by these 4our predicates. For example, Deborah and Dianne made love while Eduardo and Arturo conversed. Or Deborah made love to Eduardo and Arturo at the same time while Dianne watched. Or Dianne made love with Arturo and Eduardo at the same time while Deborah watched. The other possibility would be for Arturo and Eduardo to make love while Deborah and Dianne conversed. Or that Arturo, at the same time, first possessed one and then the other while Eduardo watched, and vice versa.

—Who did I leave out? —Asked the triangulation.

—Not me —answered the square.

—Perhaps the periphery of the 4our spirits —added the circumference.

— It's a curse to have this fire in your blood —exclaimed the mind.

—The perception of self when acting —added the topological space— fluctuates between two equally poetic universes: one outside the self, the other inside the self. The plot of this story is likely based on René Magritte's painting, The Key to Dreams. On the other hand, the distances in the macrocosm from the Earth seem to point to the past.

That is to say, in some way, we are the future of something. Or is it, perhaps, that time is relative with respect to the creation of the quantum imagination? Remember, it all started at a point in some nano universe.

It is curious that when Dianne and Arturo made love under the Gemini moon, Dianne thought of Eduardo, while Arturo thought of Deborah. And, when Eduardo and Deborah were making love under the Sagittarius moon, Deborah thought of Arturo while Eduardo was thinking of Dianne.

Distances in the microcosm seemed to point to the dreams. And dreams seemed to point to the manifestation of the void. That is, in the virtual reality of a mirror, Arturo and Eduardo made androgynous love under the Scorpio moon; Arturo thought of Dianne while Eduardo became Dianne. Simultaneously, Eduardo thought of Deborah, and Arturo became Deborah. In unison, on the other side of reality, Dianne and Deborah made androgynous love under the Taurus moon. They both thought of Aphrodite, and when Deborah thought of Dianne, Dianne became Arturo. And when Dianne thought of Deborah, Deborah became Eduardo. Then, dew, night, and enchantment sprouted from beneath the skin of all 4our.

—The distance of dreams is timeless— an ethereal voice was heard to comment. And indeed, in that instant, it happened that the almost same darkness of the night, of this night, accompanied by the moon, seemed to contemplate the nearly identical water moon of Lesbos, the almost same fire moon of Pompeii, the roughly similar mirror moon of Berkeley

—*Cogito, ergo sum*— declared René Descartes, and you, looking at the moon, kept silent. The city of Berkeley continued to be almost the same as Berkeley and the Campanile, too.

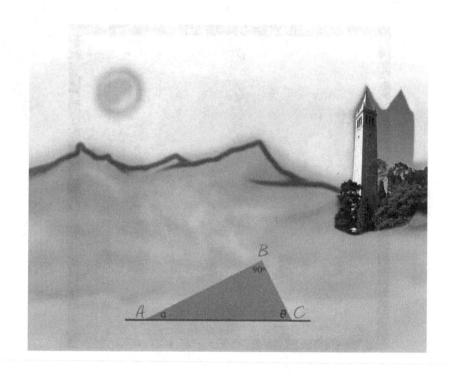

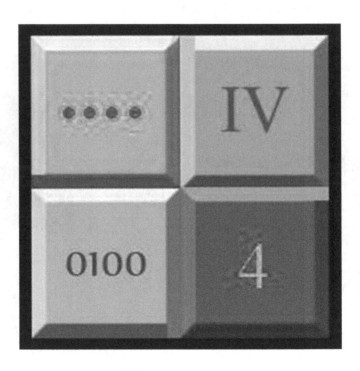

THE PHYSICAL NATURE OF THOUGHT

Narrativa
©2000 Edel Romay

In the house of memory

Memory is the theatre of the spirit

Octavio Paz[11]

*A*t the age of forty, he was living in Sausalito, California. He had made a name for himself as a fine artist, and his house, lying harmoniously on a hillside, had a beautiful view of San Francisco Bay. The psychedelic house was distributed on three uneven floors. On the first, there was the living room, the dining room, the kitchen, an extra room, the bathroom, and a sizeable overhanging terrace. On the second, downstairs, there were three unleveled bedrooms with their respective balconies and bathrooms. On the third, below the bedrooms, was a large painting studio with a private bathroom and small bar. Five steps down led to a modern courtyard leading to a Zen garden. The design was Ivan's creation. In Xalapa, Veracruz, he had graduated as an architect, a profession he never practiced because he decided to become a plastic artist. But many of his friends had been inspired by his designs.

9:00 p. m.

Brahms' Symphony No. 1 in C Minor, Op. 68 created a light and seductively slippery dreamy spell in the studio. Ivan was sitting comfortably in an armchair in front of three naked canvases. With his eyes closed and to the rhythm of the music, he tried to recreate an experience he had had at least twenty years ago when he had swallowed magic mushrooms in San Cristóbal de las Casas. «The taste of muddy mold accentuated in my mouth as I chewed them. I drank water and spit several times to the left, just as the *brujo,* Juan, had recommended. He would guide me through the labyrinths of my inner journey, so I should be calm. Georgina, my love of that time, was sitting on my right. I was

---

[11]   Weinberger, Eliot (Ed.). (1987). *The Collected Poems of Octavio Paz, 1957- 1987.* (p. 472). New York: New Direction Publishing Corporation.

sitting on the floor with my legs crossed. In front of me, the half-open door leading to the courtyard...»

A magical unfolding

Suddenly, I found myself trapped in the semicircular chiaroscuro sky formed by the oil lamp without warning. The penumbra, before the sparkling light of the wick, produced women's figures dancing, polarizing my imagination and paralyzing my body. Thoughts materialized into dancing images of bold and intense primary colors. The walls of the jacal vibrated briskly until they became powerful luminous points. I could transport myself to any moment just by thinking about it. But the darkness of the light took me by surprise, as I felt I was part of an already started watercolor—the colors mixed with mind-blowing speed. Stopping to think was eternal, and it was even more difficult to prevent my body from being kept in one place. The intensity of the colors vibrated and created filaments on my skin that immediately connected me with other dimensions. I had this strange sensation of crossing a vortex, a magical double between here and there, and then I felt like a grain of sand on a wave of the sea. I was Surfing to the sound of the waves of the chopped sea; the memories danced in a paradoxical embrace.

The echo of memory

My grandma's armchair, lenses, a cup of black coffee, and elegant living room with the traditional furniture. And those well-known voices echoing through the half-dark corridors of the vast house. Above all, that voice of a child crying, afraid, in the dark. I saw myself running across those endless hallways in darkness. And before I even thought about it, I had already transported myself to another scenario: the library and its unmistakable smell of old books lavishly lined with leather and neatly arranged on cedar shelves. The colorful stained glass accentuated that mystical light that distilled in an endless number of shades. You could smell this ancestral praise of wisdom everywhere. Three walls lined with books safeguarded the time of their day as immutable sentinels. And on the enormous mahogany desk, there was still the note that I had once left myself, in the hope that I could read it when old, perhaps, in my seventies.

The library

The library of my ancestors still resided in my memory. I was informed in the village the fire had devoured everything. What a tragedy!

The grandfather

I didn't remember grandfather, but grandmother told me in great detail how much he loved me! He wanted a son, but he would never have one. It was the horses' fault. As a young man, Grandpa had injured his testicles on horseback. But horses were still his passion «they are gods, not animals,» he used to say. He was the only one who raised blood horses in the village, the most beautiful horses you had ever seen, and he also owned the best cattle in the region. He was known as a strong character, honest, and gold heart in the area. So, when I was born, he mentally adopted me as if I were his child, knowing that my mother would not object since she was his most beloved niece. So, it was no wonder he took me for rides all over town in the afternoons on *Azabache* or *Alazán*, his two favorite horses. Other times he boasted about me in the tavern while playing cards with his friends.

Unfortunately, and without warning, my grandfather passed away during his usual afternoon nap. He died in his sleep, and he left me at the age of 18 months. The feeling of experiencing that reality again broke my heart.

So, many experiences together were suffocating me, and anguish tightened my chest like a rope tow calf.

Distances became infinite. And running was a static effort between the oscillation of things and events in *allegro non-troppo ma con brio.*

The imagination flickering

—Wait! —The Chaneque intervened—, behind the imagination, Iván Ferreira de la Puente is materializing in the region of Los Tuxtlas...

You'll see!

The scenery I'm talking about is framed in a tropical forest where enchantment, witchcraft, and seduction are as accurate as of the guava trees. Or the enigmatic taste is hidden in a small drop of pomegranate nectar. Remarkably, in this magical geometry, there are 3 equidistant cities: Santiago Tuxtla, San Andrés Tuxtla and Catemaco. That's right! Ivan was born in San Andres Tuxtla, a Colonial city surrounded by pachyderm hills adorned with various shades of green that seem to caress the sun and the full moon.

Do you smell it?

There is a symphony of aromas that combine in fruits, cinnamon, tobacco, and rum. I feel as if I were touching that unmistakable aroma of a young woman that provokes and caresses the senses. See? On the other side of the stream, she calls me under that mango tree, completely naked. The forest is perceived as provocatively young. Always green. Intoxicating and spellbinding. At the age of fifteen, I held her in my arms and loved her intensely. It was fleeting and ethereal. Her substantial attire and her indigenous features were taken away by the forest. Green glaze of green skin with well-shaped breasts of sugar-apple aroma. Her soursop lips and a jaguar-like gaze. She left amidst the thickets of the trees, carrying the echo of the macaws. That's right! The caiman, the snake, the jaguar, and the rabbits gravitate along Olmec paths. You'll see! The spell has been cast.

A pause (in brackets)

*I*van grew up all over in this green shade. He grew up amidst sunny downpours and tropical nights soaked with love and the moon. The lagoons, waterfalls, rivers, mountains, and rain designed mythological landscapes where esoteric brujos manifest themselves. These havens were the cradle of his footsteps—unconditional accomplices of his imagination. You'll see! When the monkey (*Titi*) attentively observes the rabbit contemplating the moon, you will only hear the agitated conversation of the parrots through the passive gaze of the caiman, the snake, and the jaguar. So, Ivan's entire heritage was masterfully combined in this region of women that taste tobacco, chocolate, and sugar cane.

9:36 p. m., in the study

*O*ver there, far away, as if returning from a dream, Brahms' Symphony No. 1 in C Minor, Op. 68, prompted Ivan to open his eyelids. And he opened them slowly, as slowly as a woman's gentle and delicate caress on his temples, touching his senses. He had transported himself to the times of the times; in a second, memory can take you to that eternity where time seems to have stopped because memory is the mirror of reality that constructs itself. He returned to enjoy those spaces of time for a cosmic nanosecond that remained faithful in the same landscape as back then. But imagination brought him back to the present, there, in the studio workshop, where, brush in hand, Ivan shouted: «Cabernet Sauvignon, the blood that runs, the ink that stains, may the newly-born painting grow, in this red wine of life.» And with accurate brushstrokes, he pulled on the yellows, reds, violets, greens, and blues. And he captured shades that are print on the freshly prepared canvases. Ivan heard them say: «there are chiaroscuros that do not fit in the darkness of anyone's light.» And he responded by giving masterful brushstrokes to the canvas. And behind the yellow came the orange, galloping over the ultramarine cyclopean. The instantaneous and fleeting light drew two silhouettes dancing an ancestral balance. The canvas tightened like a violin string after a high note. His temples fluttered like pigeons caught in fishing nets, and the agony of flying is reflecting in the glassy eyes of the fish caught on the beach. The sea whipped violently against the wind. Ivan set tropical storms on the canvas. The tropical storm whipping over the stained-glass windows of grandfather's library had been witnessed countless times. But now, it was different. Now he was painting the tempest drawn on a mirror and the insistent memory of that woman, the one who appeared on the other side of the river naked and caressed him with her gaze. The painting included a young girl with long cocoa-cultured legs, which tasted of chocolate and sugar cane. There were rhythms of requinto, harp, coconut, soursop, and ripe banana on the landscape. In the storm, the bougainvillea embraced the wind with fury. And the carnations fell at the sexy feet of the beautiful girl while the rosebushes grew out from Ivan's flesh. In the memory of the mirror, the tropics brought the cadence of a palm tree, the waist of a woman, a face with feline eyes, and that unmistakable taste of coffee, rum, and tobacco.

Sausalito, 1979

At dawn, a Cuban woman made love to Ivan to the rhythm of the clave and *Guaguancó*, to the taste of coconut, soursop, and ripe banana. She caressed his temples with her long hands and pianist's fingers while she lavished him with kisses and embraced him with passion. The mambo "Qué bonito y sabroso" notes took on voluptuous dimensions of mutual surrender from the radio. The love was translucent in the face of vivacious eyes and fleshy lips, and Sofia's slender body was full of fire. Sofia was also a poet by profession.

At midday

Sofia and Ivan drank chamomile tea and ate toasted bread with honey. They contemplated the San Francisco Bay from the terrace, which, sleepy and restful, stretched out along their gazes. Inside the studio, the three paintings born the night before shouted and became present as they stepped out of an enormous mirror. On the terrace, Sausalito was brimming with Spanish, mango, strawberries, and nougat. The summer afternoon fell lazily in English, while Sofia composed a poem in Spanish. In Miami, she wrote scripts in English for television. And, by the way, the poem read as follows:

Cuando partas
repartido entre dos aguas,
iré recogiendo tu imagen
anterior al viento marino

When you leave
divided between two waters,
I'll be gathering your image
before the sea wind.

The images were flickering in time.

In that instant, and not in another, the imprudent memory peered into the bottom of the mirror and found the thoughtful face of an 18-month-old boy.

Almost at the very next instant, the misguided memory peeked out for the second time at the bottom of the mirror and found the thoughtful face of a 19-year-old boy.

Almost at the same instant, before the first immediately next, the mirror deduced that memory was but time reflection. Because to forget by heart would be like wanting to rescue from my eyes the beauty of your body already forgotten by heart.

Your body,
already dissolved in my eyes,
I want to rescue it from memory.

In the recollection of memory,
I want to rescue myself from oblivion
already forgotten.

I want to forget you in oblivion,
a presence that I forget
from memory in your remembrance.

Tu cuerpo,
ya disuelto en mis ojos,
quiero rescatarlo de la memoria.

En el recuerdo de la memoria,
quiero rescatarme del olvido
ya olvidado.

Quiero ya olvidarte en el olvido,
presencia que se me olvida
de memoria en tu recuerdo.

Ivan took refuge in Sofia's arms and no longer tried to rescue those images of dancing lights from his memory. He took her in his arms and eagerly searched for her lips. The afternoon languished slowly in the Bay.

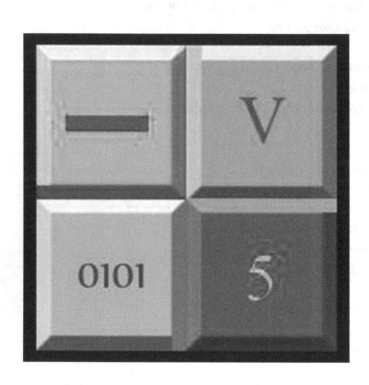

THE HOUSE OF LAVA

Narrative
©2000 Edel Romay

By the way (in parentheses)

She came from the *Levante*, from the other world. Her walk had that haughty air to it that made men leer at her. She was aware of this, and it flattered her very much. However, when these lecherous glances went from chiaroscuro to the right and left, just like a good bullfighter, she skillfully pulled out a *chicuelina*. When she walked along the San Andrés Tuxtla cobblestone streets, the stones and monoliths in the square gazed at her from top to bottom. Perhaps this is why the heavenly honey of her legs became more evident in her Greco-Roman statue features. Her serene face is framed by a pair of eyes that showed a particular ophidian mystery concentrated in her gaze. «The Mediterranean Sea has been robbed of that blue emerald pigmentation it so coquettishly displays,» his father used to say with great pride. When she wanted them to, her eyes could acquire the depth of the sea in the distance. Her mahogany hair fell straight and loose down to her lips. She has those lips whose peachy bite hinted at the eternal promised kiss. Her two-round breasts carried two tiny, suggestive erect nipples, like those of baby calves, along with an invitation to be teased. Her two slender, shapely legs gave way to a pair of beautifully shaped feet. There was a figure like a bull's head ready to charge in a bullfighting dance on the flat part of her lower abdomen. The V-shaped hair, slightly curly and also mahogany in color, protectively concealed the pulp of life. Her sex has that tuna cactus flower that invited love.

1ne

Selma Medina Soler de la Sinta, at 25, was a beautiful woman who five hundred years later would bring from Spain crazy dreams and yearnings to become a feathered snake. She studied plastic arts, but since she was a child, she was more interested in the history, stories, and legends of Los Tuxtlas.

When I was only seven years old, a neighbor had just arrived from Mexico. As he was called, Don Gervasio Ignacio Mortera Brambilla had left Spain at the age of 17teen and lived in Los Tuxtlas for 70ventys. At 88ight, he wanted to die a Spaniard, even though he felt genuinely Mexican. This curious gentleman told her entertaining fables from the area. So much so that Selma Medina, at the age of nine, was already in love with the region of Los Tuxtlas. Don Gervasio told her about the beautiful women who inhabited those hallucinogenic places and about one in particular who had stolen his heart: Antonia. He confessed that, through her, he understood the esoteric nature of Los Tuxtlas, a hidden land on the map of Veracruz. She also educated him in the art of herbal medicine. For 49 years, Antonia guided him in the *poesía bruja* of the region. Little by little and without realizing it, the spell of Los Tuxtlas entered his heart. Time stopped, memory jumped to the present, and Selma reread the first paragraph:

The Tuxtlas is an amalgam of the millennial history of the Olmecs, which later became mixed with that of the Mayans and the Aztecs. To this mixture, we can also add the indelible and easily identifiable mark left by Spain. Later, the arrival of other foreigners added more essence to the already existing cultural richness. The memory danced back in time when Selma took up the past again.

2wo

*B*etween myth and legend. Between history and fiction. The region of Los Tuxtlas became the source of life that Don Gervasio carried in his belly. His narrative was full of anecdotes. One of his favorite themes was the *fiesta brava*.

—At the beginning of the 1920s —Don Gervasio began his story— bullfighting took on a tangible furor in San Andrés Tuxtla. Look at it! — he exclaimed as his eyes filled with joy—, the bullring changed places four times. Of course, at the request of the fans! —he said proudly. At this point in the story, he paused melodramatically, and the girl followed him step-by-step. The majestic black bulls came from Nopalapan. What splendid mountain burels!

Older man and girl spent a year in that space, where the imaginary could be real, and the real, magical and dreamlike. In Selma's imagination, a fantasy created a very special *je ne sais quoi*. Full of images and symbols, Don Gervasio, on other occasions, spoke to her of «the enchanted lagoon» *and of «witchcraft»* that gravitated in dreams (of the chosen ones) when «the full moon» visited them. He explained that the witches inhabited the reality of the legend:

—To see them—he explained, opening his eyes wide—, you have to be in tune with yourself. To transmute yourself into that world is to embark on a metamorphosis.

For a year, don Gervasio filled Selma's mind with fascinating stories, where the beautiful Antonia always came out. At the age of nine, Selma asked herself the following question: «How is it that with so many beautiful women, men are not spoken of with the same enthusiasm?». And she asked herself the same question again at 19teen. At 27even, she told herself: «Male Spain found its lover in Mexico, what will female Spain find in Los Tuxtlas today?».

3hree

*T*he graduated Selma Medina Soler de la Sinta settled in Los Tuxtlas at the beginning of 1995. She went to look for the region's «male witch.» The heat of the south made her early mornings erotic, wet with sweat, tasting of mango, soursop, cocoa, and ripe papaya. She dreamt he was as a Jaguar. Eagle. Moon. Water. Jungle. She wanted him to be sensual, with a scent of cinnamon and the dampness of a fighting bull. In the architecture of dreams, she eagerly looked for him.

A medium mixture of deer and rabbit slipped into Selma's dream at the dawn of the ninth full moon. The sorcerer whispered in her ear: «Martín. Martín. Snakes turn to stone. And good Indians become Christians of the Lord. The Malinche's mongrel son rides all over the continent, infected with European blood and with problems with his color. He wants to be as white as the moon. And blond like the sunflower. Your sorcerer poet may have been lost in Latin American mythology. In this place, only traces of a millenary (human) geography remain».

At 3:00 in the morning, Selma thought she was awake. She was drenched in sweat. Then she saw herself turn left.

The room window let the full moon shine through, lighting up the naked wetness of her snake-woman shapes. Underneath her belly, orange blossoms were sprouting, half becoming fish and a half becoming blue butterflies—a specific smell of ripe fruit, American pine, and sex curdled in the air. The moon was drawn over her breasts when, on her right hand, a male shadow penetrated her. The passion was mounting on Selma's sleeping face. «There is no doubt —she said to herself— he is making love to me.» The sorcerer-poet masterfully handled the bull's head hidden between her legs. Selma, lifting her pelvis in response, repeatedly charged at the matador. Simultaneously, the sorcerer-poet whispered in her ear: « You are the feathered lady, daughter of Quetzalcoatl.»

Selma gave in to the voice of the enflamed poet in an enveloping, lethargic embrace. At noon she woke up with a crescent of feathers on her belly. Selma was more beautiful than ever. In her gaze, a moon-loving lover.

In parentheses (by the way)

*R*odrigo José Pereyra de la Torre Moreno was a 33-year-old man who lived the Mexican bourgeois lifestyle. He was very proud of his lineage, inherited from a mixture of truth, legend, and fiction. There was talk of relatives who had possessed vast fortunes amassed in gemstone businesses. There was also talk of relatives who had belonged to the upper classes but had fallen into disgrace after the French Revolution. And the most curious thing is that they spoke of Lorencillo, that bohemian pirate who stole from the English what the English, in turn, stole from the Spanish. And there was also talk of relatives who had come by boat to the coast of the state of Veracruz in 1695, at the height of what is known as *Roca Partida*, and later settled in what is now called the Moreno Peninsula.

4our

*R*odrigo was not even six feet tall. And he had that very particular Latin American presence. That's why people said that Rodrigo was handsome, with caramel-colored skin and wavy hair, in other words, very Mexican. Another of his virtues (or rarities) is that he liked to dress with a specific European elegance. Rodrigo had known how to invest his capital, and one could say that he was a man without financial problems, which allowed him to travel with ease. He was spending a month in Granada. Avignon, Bordeaux, Paris, Florence, Rome, Venice, Madrid, and Barcelona were his favorite cities. However, he also often traveled to Canada. And to the United States.

Interestingly, he also liked to dress American style. The latter was amusing to him since America is a continent. However, both in Europe and in America, he identified himself as a citizen of the world. For example, despite being born in Xalapa, he was fascinated by San Andrés

Tuxtla, the region of his ancestors. On the other hand, he claimed that both cities were his loving lovers. On the other, Quebec and Montreal in Canada were his jealous lovers. In the United States, New York, and Washington D.C. were his two favorite cities. New York, according to him, was the center of American culture. Washington D.C., according to him, was the center of international politics. He used to spend long periods in New York.

Rodrigo was a free-thinking bohemian who could be talked to for hours. Still, even for him, he emulated everything that had to do with the Renaissance for some inexplicable reason. And without losing perspective, Rodrigo also claimed that we were witnessing the beginnings of a second Renaissance. « And without losing perspective, he also claimed that we were witnessing the beginnings of a second Renaissance — he said—, the universe was understood as a text full of masterfully interwoven signs and symbols that could be decoded. At the time, astrology, magic, and alchemy represented a rediscovery of the concept of nature as a spiritual being. In the Ancient Age, somewhere between art and science, man created magic. Nowadays, somewhere between art and science, individuals create technology. In other words, in the past, man extracted the spirit from magic. Now, the individual extracts the quantum reality from technology; that is, the nano-universe of virtual reality...».

At times, when he was suffering from some existential problem or other, he would talk to his other self in a meditative and inquisitive state: «According to the Big Bang theory, all scientific evidence points out that about fourteen billion years ago, the universe of which we are now a part was in a state of absolute void, and there were no atoms. The universe was reduced to a point. «Rodrigo's imagination has no limits,» his closest friends thought. The others, those who envied him, though he was a bit «unhinged.» But Rodrigo was Rodrigo, after all.

5ive

Selma was morbidly attracted to brawny black bulls. Fighting bulls in particular. That jet-black color of furious smoothness captivated her. The recurrence of the same dream was inevitable: «A black bull comes up to me blowing softly on my sex. And as I feel the warm moisture of his breath over the nakedness of my vagina, my thighs shake to the beat of multiple orgasms».

She began to have these dreams when she was 15teen, on March 1. Most of the time, they were so real that she thought she was awake. However, at 19teen, she had a paradoxical one. She dreamt that she was awake, witnessing the dream of herself sleeping. At 5ive o'clock in the morning, she saw herself emerge from the waters of an enchanted lagoon. She was satisfied, hot, warm, and wet. On the shore, a black fighting bull was waiting for her with flamenco eyes. She faced him. She stood firm in the sand as she pulled a silver sword from her vagina. Then, raising his head, the bull roared and recited from Lorca the third stanza of the poem *"Preciosa y el Aire."* And the bull, with his tone of voice, changed and already turned into a Minotaur, sweetly whispered in her ear, while huffing and puffing: I love you.

In parentheses (the dream).

With his long tongue, the Minotaur began by kissing her lower abdomen and gradually penetrated her to the rhythm of a harp, coconut water, and the requinto. The orgasm was a breath of sea wind flavored with custard apple and ripe soursop. Then, from Selma's round breasts, two white doves sprouted and opened up like mother-of-pearl fans. Slowly the darkness fell like a naked blanket of straw, and Selma became a feathered serpent.

Since she was a child, Selma had been lucky enough to enjoy the tragedy inherent to the *fiesta brava*. In Granada, the bullring witnessed her grow up. As a child, the bullring was enormous. When she grew up, the bullring took on the stature of a cosmos in her imagination. During the bullfighting season, her father would take her to the ring. The truth is that, over the years, she learned everything there was to know about bullfighting. She was fascinated by everything that had to do with the *fiesta brava*, and she was intoxicated by it; she was transported to another world, to that world of magic, of signs, of symbolism. She would have liked to be a bullfighter. A real bullfighting lady. Bulls and death. Blood and life. Sun and sand. On an afternoon with the scent of a female, the humidity of the night, and the light of the stars.

Selma remembered the moment when she had fixed her attention on a painting in the room. She was still too young to understand the symbolism. Nevertheless, her imagination caught up with her. Even in her youth, from that dream she had at the age of 19teen, she interpreted the metaphor of the engraving. «Picasso —thought Selma out loud— mixed Greek mythology with Spanish mythology and invented a new concept: *minotauromaquia.*»

The scene that Picasso captured with such mastery in 1935 transpires by the sea. From that mysterious sea that, by looking at it so much, she carried in her eyes. The engraving remained there, beyond her memory; there, in the subconscious. And the scene took and kept taking on a life of its own in her imagination. Selma remembered that on the right side of the image is a vast Minotaur. As a teenager, such an appearance aroused in her not only a particular slight fear but, at the same time, a specific provocative and robust sexual attraction. The Minotaur advances towards a young girl who responds to an intoxicating inner call of fear and pleasure with a slow and threatening pace. This girl-woman holds a lit candle in her left hand and a bouquet in her right. She is waiting for the Minotaur. Right behind the young girl, a bearded, half-naked man is climbing quickly up a ladder. Between the young girl and the Minotaur, a horse, trapped by terror, carries a woman bullfighter with a sword in her right hand in the painting center. The woman is dressed as a bullfighter, with an unbuttoned shirt and a pair of beautiful breasts. In the air, the breasts look like two full moons. Above, on the upper left, two young women, each holding a white dove, attentively watch what is happening below.

"Selma thought out loud again— the scene attempts to illustrate the cyclical dance of Thanatos and Eros.»

It was no coincidence that in 1989, after that lascivious dream, she bought herself Picasso's picture book *Bacanales, mujeres, toros y toreros* for her birthday.

«What a coincidence! —Selma thought out loud—, in that same 1970 when I was born in Granada, Picasso donated almost all his early work to the Barcelona museum». Picasso, like her, was born at midnight, under a full moon, on October 25.

Pablo Ruiz (Picasso) was born in 1881, in Malaga. Federico García Lorca was born on June 5, 1898, n Fuente Vaqueros. The surprising thing about all this is that all three of them were equally passionate about bullfighting.

6ix

On December 31, 1995, Selma and Rodrigo met at the New Year's Eve Ball in San Andrés Tuxtla. It was at midnight. Between the hugs and toasts to wish everyone a «Happy New Year.» The light of the crescent moon caressed the region and accentuated the small noises of the night. The tropical music in the dance hall bathed the bodies of the dancers with its sensual notes. The rhythm sailed on the magic candor of musical instruments. It was in the cadenced, ancient, and intoxicating *danzón* that Rodrigo dared to dance with her. Selma followed him into the ring without any resistance. Antonio María Romeu's *danzón*, *La flauta mágica* brought them and carried them with the flavor of palm trees, coconut and ripe guava. The night exhaled a hot, sensual, and intoxicating wet mist. The *La mora danzón,* by Barbarito Diez, became intimate. Their bodies drew closer and then further to the rhythm of their legs, which traced accurately executed steps. The sweat from their bodies drew a bullfighting dance. Selma imagined herself to be a bullfighter and felt Rodrigo as a Minotaur. At that precise moment, Rodrigo, with both hands, took her by the waist and drew her closer to his body. Selma narrowed her eyes and thought of Picasso's engraving. Rodrigo pressed her gently against his wet chest. And he felt the sharp edge of those two erect nipples searching for her skin behind her humid blouse, her two round breasts floating between the hot moisture of their sweat and that violent urge to be squeezed by the Minotaur's lips. Selma closed her eyes and felt that liquid wetness between her legs. And she imagined the warmth of her sex between Rodrigo's moist lips.

They danced until dawn. They went out together at 5ive in the morning, holding each other by the waist, talking and laughing excitedly. The fresh morning air fell slowly on their wet faces. They got into Rodrigo's jeep and headed for the road to Catemaco. At 5:15teen, to their amazement, they were at the *Laguna Encantada*. Rodrigo did not forgive himself for such a distraction. And at that instant, Selma just then remembered the dream she had had in Spain: «The Minotaur was waiting for me at the edge of a pond while I emerged naked from the water... *Dèja vu* can be a terrifying experience», she told herself.

Rodrigo looked at her with the eyes of a Minotaur; she looked back at him with her eyes filled with the Mediterranean Sea. Rodrigo kissed her breasts, which, behind the unbuttoned shirt, were trembling with fire. Those erect nipples, the color of damson plum, attacked Rodrigo's lips, tasting honey, orange blossom, and incense. In turn, Selma, with her fleshy lips, kissed his temples, where a pair of horns carved with serpentine moonlight were sprouting. They hurriedly undressed and, on a blanket woven by indigenous craftswomen's hands that Rodrigo had brought in the jeep, they lay down on the dewy grass. In the labor of love, they performed different «cape and muleta passes.» And almost at the end of a «natural,» they switched to the Kama Sutra. At 7:20wenty a.m., wet with dew, sweat, and love, they were caught in the gaze of a witch-boy who watched the moon move away at the arrival of the Tuxleco sun.

Selma and Rodrigo dressed lazily, climbed into the jeep, and left for Catemaco for the second time. In Quezalapan, already in Rodrigo's house, they drank orange juice and ate papaya with lemon. On the stereo, he picked out the CD called *El danzón*. The music was flooding the air as they undressed. They took a warm shower. Then they got into an enormous water bed, where they made love for the umpteenth time. In front of the bed, there was a stained-glass window in which the dominant color was blue. On the other side of the window, Catemaco was drawn floating on a crystal lagoon.

The source (in parentheses)

Selma, through Don Gervasio, had bought a colonial residence in San Andrés Tuxtla. The house, like the region, held myth and geography: legend and history. Be warned! In this house, metamorphosis and transmutation occurred daily. The courtyard, in particular, was a work of art in local plant medicine gardening. Selma also dotted around stone and clay sculptures masterfully designed by Selma. The courtyard was a perfect square where the pottery acquired its most extraordinary splendor. In the center was a round fountain in which four cobbled diagonals converged. Surrounding the courtyard, with their respective arches, were four corridors. Selma's bedroom had a stained-glass window with blue and yellow as the primary colors on the second floor. A yellow quilt covered the vast round bed in the center. The moonlight reached her bed in the early morning, coming in through the terrace and then the stained-glass window. It was the sixth morning of 1996, and I was going to illuminate Chalchihuitlicue, the beautiful woman of the waters. The rite and the symbol are intermingled with history and legend. This magical sanctuary lived an ecological sorcerer, half tradition and half modernity, which is why Selma had decided to design this fountain, which looked more like an enchanted lagoon. The site was decorated with solid colors; the greens, yellows, reds, violets, and blues stood out. In the center of the fountain, on a bundle of snakes, a statue of a naked woman was opening her arms to a Minotaur. At night, the fountain is lit up. At noon, the water lilies floated restlessly.

By the way (in parentheses), for dinner

San Andrés is about 160 km from the port of Veracruz, but Selma went there specially to buy good Spanish wine, preserves, and cooking ingredients, not to mention, of course, the delicious ham. She had set her mind to cooking something very Spanish. And very much from Veracruz. So, she left early and went home in the afternoon. It was worth the trip. Besides, it was a way to break the routine she had imposed on herself.

7even

A bottle of Faustino, I from 1989, rested patiently on the coffee table in the large room decorated by Selma. Next to it, two elegant Mexican wine glasses. They were olives, Manchego cheese, slices of Iberian ham, and garlic toast on an oval plate. On another equally elegant dish were mussels and potatoes in green sauce. And yet on another platter, chicken in yellow mole, peas, and chayote. The stereo played Ottmar Liebert's music over and over again. The ambiance was very relaxed and horny.

Rodrigo poured two glasses of red wine, and they toasted with a silent gesture. After the first sip, they both thought they heard a bell and a bull roar coming from the courtyard. They stared into each other's eyes and said nothing. The music made the night more intimate, cadenced, and voluptuous. At the beginning of the third cup, Selma made a toast to herself (she had finally found the sorcerer poet, that enigmatic man she had so often dreamed of). Both were silent as they listened to the music on the stereo. The immensity of the night, helped by the music, reached the senses like an erotic massage.

—Agustín Lara composed a song dedicated to your hometown — said Rodrigo, breaking the silence.

—Of course! —responded Selma flirtatiously—, do you want to listen to it?

—Yes! —Rodrigo exclaimed—, us Jarochos used to sing to you before we even met you.

She kissed him and went to the wall-mounted wardrobe with shelves and glass doors, where she kept the old long play records. She picked out the selection entitled *Un poco de mis sentimientos*, original songs by Agustín Lara, looked at it with tenderness and, addressing Rodrigo, by way of explanation, said:

—When I turned 9ine, Don Gervasio gave me this collection. She lovingly chose the album 3res, side 1no, *Granada*, and placed it in the stereo. Agustín Lara's *Granada* was heard loud and melodious in Alejandro Algara's voice. Both of them paid close attention to the lyrics, which they already knew by heart. And they could imagine the way the Veracruz lyrics crossed the sea to Granada. «Oh, Granada! —Rodrigo thought—, so close and so far from the sea. And as if Selma had heard his thoughts, she answered:

—Of course! But for the massive barrier of the Sierra Nevada.

—In Granada, I could feel that ancestral longing for the sea in the air —said Rodrigo—. Lorca explained it perfectly in his poetry.

—Bravo! —interrupted Selma with overflowing joy and, adopting a gypsy stance, recited what he remembered of the *Romance de la pena negra*.

Breathless, both toasted the Andalusian universe, a mixture of native Andalusia, and the subsequent immigration of Jews, Arabs, gypsies. And for witnessing the coming of the second Renaissance. Rodrigo and Selma were finally toasted to having met 5ive years after the change of year, decade, century, and millennium. They felt that they were characters from other worlds and other times. But they didn't say anything. Yet, they laughed with contagious joy. They talked, of course, about philosophy, history, and art. They discussed their very personal views on myth, legend, magic, and witchcraft. At the same time, they talked a lot about the social commitment of science, technology, literature, cinema. But they didn't talk about their real fears. Rodrigo said nothing, for example, about the terror and anxiety that the full moon provoked in on some nights. Selma didn't say much about her dreams, either, often waking up during full moon nights.

With a bottle and a half of Faustino I and a good portion of tapas inside, Selma suggested they proceed to the dining room. Spacious and elegant, it combined that classic touch of comfort and functional austerity. The elegance of the cedar furniture belonged to the second half of the 18th century. The dining table comfortably accommodated 6ix people. The outstanding detail of the dining room were the 7even brands, styles, and ages of wall clocks, which showed 7even different times. One of the 7even times that Rodrigo identified quickly was that of San Andrés Tuxtla. The second of Granada. The third Tibet. The fourth of Jerusalem. The remaining three remained a mystery. Although Rodrigo insisted several times, Selma refused to tell him.

8ight

*T*he paintings in the room, unlike the sculptures, reminded Rodrigo of the magical, dreamlike style of Remedios Varos. But the images had been recently painted by Selma. «Like that of Remedios Varos—Rodrigo thought—, Selma's art is motivated and animated by childhood myths. There is a certain enigmatic oneiric correspondence —he argued with himself— between reason and Selma's fantastic reality». Rodrigo was so caught up in the internal conversation that he didn't immediately realize Selma's asking him. He didn't hear the question until the third time:

—What do you think of the leg of lamb? —Exquisite —he answered—, but I prefer yours —he added jokingly. There was a little silence. Then Selma, as if Rodrigo had guessed the thought, explained:

—In my work, I seek a balance between reason and myth. My creativity fluctuates between a dream world and quantum geometry. The commitment of intelligence, as an artist, is to be at the service of sensitivity. Not everything that we see is quantifiable.

Rodrigo, looking lost in the distance and as if he were somewhere else in another dimension, took a solemn drink of wine, wiped his mouth with his napkin, and answered:

—The possible worlds of the imagination can be made real through action. The productive power of the transcendental imagination is precisely that magical space that mixes history and fiction. Time only exists in human perception.

There was a thick silence in the dining room that both of them took advantage of to pour more wine, look each other tenderly in the eyes, and kiss each other with a new passion. Then, they served each other for the second time with the exquisite leg of lamb. At midnight, they finished the third bottle of Faustino I. For dessert, there was mango ice cream, cheese, fruit, and more Faustino I. The background music by Ottmar Liebert, which had so appropriately accompanied the dinner, was replaced by B-Tribe. This new rhythm helped to intensify their caresses.

By the way (in parentheses), the moon

*T*he full moon entered the room and crawled gently into the sky-blue sheets on the bed. There, in all their intimacy, it illuminated the interlocking volume of two naked bodies. On the vast round bed, a lady bullfighter performed cape and muleta's passes to the rhythmic onslaught of a Minotaur. The Minotaur had two horns carved with feathered snakes. The dawn with the taste of fruit and dew remained hidden between two panting bodies that spun with love. In the courtyard, the bellowing of a bull and the rattling of a snake was heard. Above the fountain, the statue of a woman and the Minotaur became one single interlocking statue. The house's corridors, the courtyard, and the fountain were impregnated with moon, music, ocote, and incense.

Selma and Rodrigo entered the dream universe of an artist that morning. The witnesses to this story are the house, the city, and the region of Los Tuxtlas.

—In 24our hours, dawn can be eternal —said the butterflies.

—The cobwebs are pearly with dew —pointed out the lizard.

—The night before tomorrow night —added the sorcerer —she will be pregnant.

9ine

Selma painted a picture in a house with white walls and orange roofs on the essential living room wall. This ontological space frames metamorphosis, legend, and transmutation. The painting is called *El minotauro a orillas de la laguna encantada posee a una hermosa joven y la deposita desnuda sobre la hierba húmeda* (The minotaur on the banks of the enchanted lagoon ravishes a beautiful young woman and lays her naked on the wet grass).

In the courtyard, inside the round fountain, and veiled by water lilies, a disembodied voice tells a brief story:

—In this house of ecological colors, when the full moon arrives expressly to visit, the inhabitants of the Los Tuxtlas region believe to remember having seen a boy of 9ine years that entered and left the painting that lives and gravitates on the most important wall of the living room.

The old ladies say they saw him playing in the courtyard.

— In truth, the child has a sharp, penetrating jaguar look, a flamenco rhythm, and cinnamon-colored eyes.

That and more is what the villagers are saying. And if you still doubt it, ask the shadows of the house! Yes, the ones that appear in the chiaroscuro foliage of the courtyard and the fountain. See! Quantum geometry here has intersected oneiric geometry.

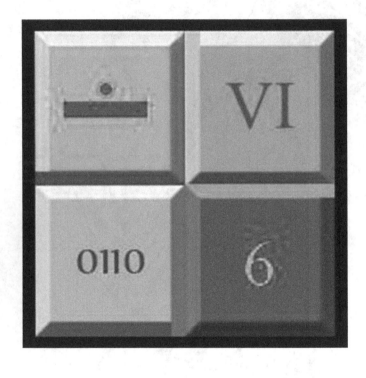

THE REFLECTION OF WATER

Narrative

© 2001 Edel Romay

IMPORTANT NOTE

*L*et me tell you a story that, true as it is, you will think is a lie. Oh my! Well then, let me tell you a lie, which, true as it is, you will think is a story.

— I agree!
— A story is not a mere abstraction of reality.
— So, what is it, then? — You asked vehemently.
— It is another reality — I replied.
— Parallel? — You asked me.

— No! Well, not necessarily. Instead, they are intertwined realities like the ones I am about to tell you. Now pay attention to my words. Life on the planet originated in the depths of the sea, most likely near some thermal hole where chemical substances could be combined that, little by little, produced the first simple cells. It is said that this task began at least 3.5 billion years ago. And it took Mother Nature at least 2.5 billion years to produce multicellular life. Wait a minute! I already see your expression of amazement, and I agree with you: seen from our perspective as humans, it was a very slow-moving task, but not so for the cosmic entities. If you are still interested in the subject, I suggest you look for the origin of life on Earth on Google. Of course, man's evolution was equally slow. You will see. What I can assure you is that human beings have some amphibians in them. Of course! We were shaped in the same way as images become integrated into a water mirror. Have you noticed how similar a pregnant woman's belly is to the planet Earth? Yes, a woman's womb, like the planet, also gives life. Incidentally, both you and I were shaped inside a water bubble.

And an ethereal voice was heard shouting: Salty seawater «Agua salá.» A nocturnal ejaculation. The sea. And in the silence of zero, Woman Creation reached one. She then kept silent so that the night would continue to advance until slowly merged with the dawn.

COSMIC TRANSCENDENCE

«Matter has an expiration date,» concluded Cronos mixing time with space, 3113 years BC, while igniting the human brain with a spark of dark energy... Then, following a cosmic moment, Zeus' turn, who proclaimed himself a god in due course, declared himself a god and erased his father from the landscape. Already in Olympus, as the supreme god, he came down to Earth from time to time to seduce mortals. One of the mortals he seduced was called Semele, who would engender Dionysus. In his passionate copulation with Semele, Zeus thought: «There will be 3hree women and a goat under the May moon». Just then, Zeus noticed that flora and fauna besides the cliff stealthily invaded Pan's dream. The goat, in panic, dreamed that it would quickly climb up the cliff rocks until it reached the forest, where three nymphs covered with flowers danced under the moonlight. Dionysus seemed to meditate on the mahogany table, and his fingers played with a cup of carved clay. All this was going on in Zeus' mind as he copulated with Semele.

IN A TIME, BUBBLE

—Am I dreaming? —Murmured Sebastián.

—I believe (Creo), I create (Creo), I think (Creo), 3hree different women's voices replied. And the three women's voices fell to the cliff at the very moment a hummingbird sucked the nectar out of the flowers. In the comings and goings of the waves on the rocks, a sensual chant merged below. Just then, the echo, freeing itself from the void, exclaimed:

— I believe, I create, I think.
—Am I dreaming? — Murmured Sebastian.
— I believe (Creo). I create (Creo). I think (Creo)—the same 3hree women's voices replied.

At the same time, the sea continued to embrace the rocks uselessly, and, in doing so, it melted into an infinite number of bubbles. The spectacle was both imposing and marvelous. The dawn was meticulously dyeing the image in an endless watercolor of brilliant colors. In that instant, in that silence of silence itself, where the nuances took on their most extraordinary splendor, in that entropy of dawn, Sinatra's voice was heard singing *That's Life*.

«Am I dreaming?» Sebastián asked himself.

I CONFESS

My obsession with mixing music with landscape led me to configure a binary reality: theirs and mine. In other words, the genuineness was associated with the icon when it evoked and invoked subtleties such as «she was magical» or «she was lewd,» or «she was innocent.» Perhaps, spiritual and inexplicable as quantum reality. Because names followed the images of this reality, and when I invoked them, they evoked universes full of cosmic dreams. The curious thing is that, in the dynamics of my memory, none of them was fixed or isolated; on the contrary, each one seemed to have certain autonomy to interfere with my memories. In my urge to know them, I once invented them; and they probably once created me. Memory then fell into the abyss of an interactive and virtual space, and I could no longer distinguish them. As in the sea, the waters mixed between the wind and the cliff; however, they were just in the autonomous moment of their existence in the abyss of memory. And so, they arrived, charging with the potential of a static dynamic. Non-Euclidean geometric invocation with a taste of nostalgia and saltwater. They came, one by one when I called them, and they landed, one by one, among my feelings. Then I perceived myself on the mahogany table, catching lascivious waves of salt and charm.

The names I will evoke and invoke are not the same, nor are they real. They have a sequential order of appearance; they are waves oscillating possibilities; they are images that update a reality. The actual names are engraved on the reef, where the locks are cut by song.

AND THE VOICE FELL FACE UP AND MERGED WITH THE SUN

Amanda

—Sofía — a voice was heard.
—Amanda — an echo was heard to reply.

And in the echo of the cliff, a silhouette was heard to shout:

—Sofía, Amanda.

That slender woman with long legs and hawkish gaze. The boastful and sensual one, who openly presumed to be a bird and a fairy, because being a witch, she said, implied connotations she did not like. She came from the Southern Cone, bathed in a lethargic dream of sea and mountains, the poetry of snow in the heights, and poetry of saltwater on the beach. Chilean and daring, there are many songs and bursts of light in the constellated air when a poem by Neruda explodes.

One morning, listening to Brahms, Symphony No. 2 in D major, opus 73, I caressed his back from top to bottom, smooth as the back of a Cimarron cat, while, in unison, I recited a single verse of Neruda in her ear:

—«I can write the saddest verses tonight.»

Surrendered at the pinnacle of orgasm, she whispered in my ear

—Pablo.

Then, between kisses and caresses, I baptized her with the name of Sorceress Witch. And she, in turn, called me Catullus, the faun lost in a forest of glass.

She was with me for barely a month. And for not-so-obvious reasons, she refused to explain why she trapped time in such a Euclidean space: A month. It could well have been an eternity or the angular flight of a condor when it falls from the heights, down the Andes, and melts into the immensity of the sea when it kisses the sky. It could have been, perhaps, a sigh or eight seconds in the entire duration of a dream. I am not sure, but it could also have been the caress of the wind on the branches of my thoughts. I remember every day. But my most vivid memories are of Saturday nights, under the flickering light of the candles and bathed by the erotic and intense incense. Then, after three glasses of well-served Greek Retsina wine and a delicious Greek dinner, Amanda, to my delight, performed and danced *Catulli Carmina*. Because of Carl Orff's *Trionfi* triptych, *Catulli Carmina* pierced her to the bottom of her soul. It was that, as if by magic, all of a sudden, she, the Chilean Amanda, was reincarnated as Clodia, that beautiful Roman woman who had captivated the love of the poet Cayo Valerio Catullus. It was then that, naked, she danced torch in hand all over the house, behind an ethereal lover. Behind the lighted candles, I could feel Eros take on quantum rhythm dimensions. At that moment, imitating a Dionysian dance, Clodia met Catullus again. I, already converted into Catullus, without being able to avoid it, she turned me into a satyr under her intense gaze. She, before me, turned into a nymph and surrendered.

We danced until dawn. And at the pinnacle of fantasy, we both entered the forest of pleasure shortly before a dew sheet pearled our skin. Tear-flavored mist, the gentle murmur of waves, your body vibrating. Lethargic geometry of quantum logic. The geometry of the sea with the wind. The geometry of your lips. Saltwater symphony on the reef. Poetry of snow in the heights. A tear was running down your cheek.

I searched the landscape for a trace of her absence even before she left. Time wanted to stop quickly in the morning, like the deceptive illusion of seeing water on the horizon of the desert. But I could feel the emptiness she had left me. Perhaps that is why, in our brief encounter, I chose to stop time when I caressed her face with jungle water while she joined me with the angular surrender of a condor—my beloved sorceress nymph, floating naked in my imagination.

AND THE VOICE FELL FACE DOWN AND MERGED WITH THE SEA

Mónica

—Selma — the echo was heard to reply.
—Mónica — a voice was heard to call out.

*A*nd in the crashing of the waves on the rocky cliffs, an echo was again heard to shout:

—Selma, Mónica.

Tango, *bandoneon*, *pampa*, *piano*, *gaucho* and south stave. Malambo of light brown skin, I believe it, with a taste of Carlos Gardel, Atahualpa Yupanqui, Leonardo Favio and Facundo Cabral. Although *porteña*, the immensity of Argentina took her to the surface —geography of vast horizons—. Seeing her dance tango was like capturing, in a single second, the speed of the fish or the angular flight of birds of the Pampa. The long/tall rhythm of a slender girl's body (*Lunga cadenciosa de cuerpo de ragazza esbelta*); erotic, daring, fleeting, violent, and rhythmic silhouette, with a taste of permanence, contact, and elasticity. To converse with her was to park on the notes of a bandoneon with voice and song.

I met her accidentally during the summer. And I say accidentally because I did not plan to attend Malena's party that Friday. Hanging in my dining room, the hours went by anonymously and imperceptibly until, in a blink, I realized that the clock in the dining room marked 10:00 at night. I took the black corduroy sack and, driving my red Mustang, and I went to Malena's place. The pretentious blonde Malena lived in Berkeley in a Californian-style house leaning against a hillside. Striding up the cobblestone stairs leading to the main entrance, I came across a well-proportioned ass of a slender tall girl body (*derriere de ragazza lunga*), trapped inside tight black corduroy trousers. However, my attention was rapt when I discovered a pair of delicate and sensual feet flying uphill, very much despite being imprisoned, temporarily, in a couple of high-heeled sandals of triple-banded mahogany leather. The long, flirtatious fingers had their nails painted terracotta, and they seemed to know that the sandals emphasized a certain fetishism hidden in the senses. I was first provoked, and I felt a vivid and savage urge to kiss them all over. But my eyes rose to the off-white silk shirt, which, subtle and provocative, revealed a thin torso with narrow shoulders and a pair of small rounded breasts. At eye level, I could feel that look languid but equally penetrating. That pair of feline eyes were nailed to me in a Dionysian dance, accompanied by a face of fine lines. And the fleshy O-shaped lips asked me:

—Hello, what is your name?
—Sebastián, Sebastián Mortera —I answered—. And you, what is your name?
—Mónica Giarnelli.

That night, half the attendees at Malena's house assumed that Monica was my partner; the other half probably inferred that I was her partner. Whatever it was, we went in together and presented ourselves with an informal «Hello!» to which those closest to us replied with an equally casual «Hi!» After the handshakes and kisses on the cheeks, I noticed that most of them talked enthusiastically, while the rest seemed to pay special attention to the milonga emitted, wet and hot, by the stereo. Coming back from the kitchen with two glasses of red wine, to my surprise, everyone had left an open space of fixity and vertigo for Monica and her dance partner in the large living room. The atmosphere was heavy with music, with notes loaded with tight body substance. Angular, straight, oblique, and cosmic, the bandoneon was presented with sorrow, pain, desire, and life, like a sigh that sought the pretext of making itself present by flying fast and letting itself fall slowly. Light as a young and agile lioness, as a nervous gazelle, Monica stuck to the sensual and enigmatic rhythm. In that symbology of notes and silhouettes, the couple became one and then two bodies, with fleeting legs, intertwining voids of musical tempo and dis-tempo languidly slow and other times fast like flocks of constellated birds in an open universe. Monica's womanly shapes tore out flames from deep inside me. Her feet were snatching my gaze while her cadenced and lascivious float continued among the notes of the tango night. The tango looked for the moss of the skin, explored the sensual flavor of form. Her feet claimed time and space. The fluttering of those feet received a sweet impulse of a ring of fish floating in the waters of a starry sea.

After my well-planned strategies to isolate Monica from the conversation and company hoarders who never miss a get-together, the opportunity presented itself as she crept away from the room and, elusive, went out alone to the terrace for some air. I approached her, taking care of my lexicon so as not to bore her nor sin unwary. The exchange of words was fluid. I congratulated her on her doctorate in Comparative Literature from the University of California at Berkeley. And I did not know how to respond when dismayed, she told me about her separation from her husband Mario, just as she was writing the last chapter of her dissertation. And, despite everything, she was still living in the Villa (The University Village, in Albany). At about 1:30 in the morning, perhaps to change the whoopee (*quilombo*), she invited me to escape from the party to get a hamburger. I immediately took her up on the idea, and, already in my car, I suggested we go to the Mexicalli Rose in Oakland. She warned me that she did not eat spicily and that she knew very little about Mexican food. Naked in front of her curious and flirtatious gaze, I confessed to her that I considered myself a painter, a poet, and a writer, but that, for financial reasons, I worked as a bureaucrat for an engineering company in the city of San Francisco.

— *Che*! —She said with her melodic *porteño* accent— What are you complaining about? You have work. — He kept talking, but I could not pay attention to what she was saying anymore; I was stunned. I regained my five senses when I heard, clearly:

—Come, let us go home.

The journey from Oakland to Albany was concise; when I realized we were in the Villa and Monica was opening the door to her apartment. The tour was fun and fast. On the left, the room with plants hanging a foot away from the window. Perpendicular and glued to the wall, a comfortable white sofa with its corresponding coffee table. In front of the couch, a Fisher stereo close to the wall. To the right, the dining room kitchen. Opposite, at the end of a narrow corridor, is the bathroom. On the left, the bedroom, a queen-size bed, and a wooden imitation Viennese rocking chair. To the right, the other bedroom, which they had initially used as a library. She instinctively said, «we use,» but immediately corrected herself:

—Now, «I use» it as a work and study room.

She offered me mate back in the hall while putting on Astor Piazzolla: *La Historia del tango*, volume 2. Mónica, squatting in front of the stereo, her *derrière* incited me unreservedly, for the third time, to paint it with fauvist brushstrokes. As she turned and found my face bewildered by the fact that I did not know what mate was, she took me by the hand gently and, laughing mockingly, made me stand up, grabbed me by the waist, and led me to the kitchen. Piazzolla's sensual notes were beginning to set in the air.

—Look —she said—, this is a cured calabash, this is a *bombilla* and this is the mate. You put the *yerba* in the calabash and add hot water little by little. But you have to wait a couple of minutes for it to be ready.

While she waited patiently, leaning on my left shoulder, for the chemistry of water to release the essence of yerba mate. I, millimeters away from her well erect breasts, was content (for the moment) only to compare them with the almost round geometry of the two calabashes with their respective buttons that, from under her blouse, challenged my most genuine intentions to make them into mate.

—Now — she continued to take the calabash and draw the end of the bombilla closer to her lips — you take a sip of the infusion. —And, putting the calabash in my hands, she extended the bombilla to my lips.

We repeated this ritual several times. The bombilla traveled the increasingly shortened distance from her lips to mine. The full flavor of the mate, the humid radiation of her body, her womanly scent, the music, the tango, all this and more prompted me also to sip mate from her lips. She did not resist; on the contrary, she, agile and firm, was sticking to my body. Her half-opened lips gave me a mate-flavored kiss back, eyes closed and a burst of furtive caresses. Without haste, she began to fit around my body, stopping here and there as if recognizing the erect topography of my passion. Meanwhile, her skin was springing sea mist as I licked it. Between my legs, trapped in her mouth, swam restless fish. It was then that I realized that, from the very beginning, the seducer had not been me.

We turned off the lamps to make way for the dawn light. Already in the bedroom, we received the diaphanous clarity of the dawn that surprised the *Noche de Amor* to the rhythm of Piazzolla. Our lips on each other's skin brought murmurs, heartbeats, dew, torrents, transparent syllables, cascades of fire, uncontrollable groans of pleasure. The dawn light, helped by my caresses, slowly transformed Monica's brown skin, which took on shades of blue, yellow, green, orange, violet, and terracotta, accentuating her womanly shapes in a multicolored swarm of chiaroscuro. Like ten tiny little fish, Monica's toes succumbed deliciously one by one to my love bites. Then my lips ran over her ankles, legs, and thighs, rediscovering, again and again, the Hellenic architecture of her sculptural legs. And, having become a faun, I entered the vertex of her sex. Sea flavored seashells touched my lips, moss, and port wind with my 5ive tongues; I was feeling the nautical rose of her ocean. And there was a tidal wave of liquid suns coming from 5ive directions at the same time. Discovering planes and volumes, I found myself in the Pampa of her belly, where little by little I was transfiguring into a gaucho and slowly and avidly drank the mate of her serene breasts.

Her two erect nipples danced malambo between my thirsty lips. Finally, I climbed up to her neck with my lips open, very close to her ear, and amidst moans of pleasure, I whispered: —I died! —As I sank into her body, there was an echo of a milonga at the pinnacle of a summer dawn.

Exhausted at six in the morning, we submerged into a deep aquatic sleep. I gave Mónica one of my paintings in exchange for the emptiness she would leave me with and did not want to take with her. She gave me the calabash, the bombilla, and a packet of yerba mate. Monica was like this: a milonga dream. Monica was with me 17teen days, 17teen morningless days, 17teen magical dawns, 17teen timeless hours, 17teen saltwater dreams. That is what Monica was like.

At dawns like this one, drinking mate, I hear her with my gaze floating with her tanned legs. She appears like Botticelli's Venus, sweating molasses. And the taste of her skin, the memory, and what is now my sadness tears my heart out. However, when I play Gardel, *Mi querido Buenos Aires*; or Facundo Cabral, *Hermano regresa a casa*; or Atahualpa Yupanqui, *Milonga del solitario*; or Leonardo Favio, *Mi tristeza*, with my five senses, my soul, in the words of Neruda, "is not content to have lost her."

AND THE VOICE FLOATED IN THE AIR AND CONJUGATED ITSELF...

Tatiana

—Lydia —a voice was heard calling.
—Tatiana —replied the echo.

*P*resto, the day told the night:

—The names engraved on the cliff are made of *Viento Entero*.

The wind, leaving behind a haze of poetry, rode on the horizon.

If I remember rightly, Paz, in his poem entitled Eternal Whole Wind (*Viento Entero*), said: «the present is perpetual.» Perhaps that is where the esoteric of my confession lies, but I have no doubt! Simply, like the electron, I find myself suspended in the very place where the times of the times are conjugated. There where, by empathic suggestion, infinite realities are created. And I find myself there without knowing how to distinguish between the past and the future. However, the possibility of it «having happened tomorrow» is imminent. The important thing is that it happened simultaneously in Madrid and Montreal, Mexico and San Francisco, Paris, and Lima.

The truth is that music does not measure distances, nor, I think, does memory measure time. The most likely thing is that I created Tatiana playing the guitar. I did not show up at the concert or after the social gathering in her honor. It had to have been on the other side of dreams, where memories are present, where the forest becomes spring, and the rocks of the river mix with the waters. Because at this moment, the amber color of her curly hair is between my lips, and the tan skin of her naked, voluptuous body of a bronze statue is in my hands.

What am I saying! Tatiana wrapped in white sheets, guitar in hand, playing Paganini's *Veinticuatro caprichos in guitar*. «Paganini in guitar?» I asked myself, surprised. My intrigue was cleared up later when Tatiana told me about the legend and controversy caused by Paganini's relationship with the guitar. Once she had played Oscar Avilés and Pepe Torres, I also found out that she was a Young Peruvian woman who did not settle for just playing select music. That morning, dressed in music, we made love.

She fast, running distances.
Me, letting the sea breeze lead me softly to her sex, where the compass rose eternally laid.
She, fire on the furnace. Me, a fish in water.
She, the whole eternal wind. Me, the sea.
She is poetry: me, verse.
She, 23. Me, 52.

At the exact moment of orgasm, I sensed that the illusory future was blocking the way to yesterday, in the already rapid indecisive dimension of the present. It was a revealing interval in which I believe I have seen moons resembling the breasts of nymphs. Or white pigeons are playing with firefish. Then, the landscape on the other side of my senses painted symphonic notes where mighty rivers cascaded down the mountain. That is to say, the inevitable happened, memory became present, and memories took on a memory of their own. For example, Tatiana today is a chestnut filly that frolics among a plethora of erotic notes.

Intriguingly, when we caress each other, I perceive myself entering the mountains and seas of emotions, where I can taste sea salt in Tatiana's dewy sweat. And the sea in Tatiana's tears becomes human. All the moisture of her skin is conjugated in my sweat and my tears because I cried tomorrow today. Because yesterday tomorrow came edited today. Because the body is subject to time and space. Because the present is perpetual. And the misfortune of memory is that it does not know how to measure distance. Because to conjugate the tense of the adequate verb, we must resort to the perpetual habit of the present.

Tatiana, I helplessly explore each one of your shapes with my lips. And it just so happens that the most impressive thing about your face is your mouth. And of your body, that perfect pair of legs. But anticipating my desires, slowly, your almond, mischievous and lively eyes explore my senses far below your gaze. They captivate me and pull inaccessible songs from me.

It is true! The illusion of time is waiting. And when the time comes, your long hands like magic birds will make me hear quantum landscapes: the guitar. The guitar, visceral space of 6ix strings. The guitar, circular space where the senses ride. The guitar, absence, and the shape of a woman where pain becomes a sigh. The guitar, staff full of ethereal notes. The guitar, space of strings, and 6ix temperate knives are tearing my soul. The guitar turned into Tatiana takes away my memory. And the inevitable happens: Tatiana's skillful hands, turned into fiery birds, burn my senses. The memory realized in Tatiana becomes infinite. And my soul went mad looks for it 3hree times in π, crossing the 6ix strings simultaneously. The circle explodes in my viscera, and the melody drags me to its encounter.

EPILOGUE

*I*n North America, at the intersection between a memory and a dream, South America adhered to a cliff. The sequoias forest soon made a sketch. In the noise of silence. In the very sting of silence. There where the nuances increased to become only shadows in that silence. In that evening's entropy, Sinatra's voice was heard singing My Way. Listen!

There was a vast, white-walled house above the cliff, where the May moon seemed to challenge the space conceived in a grain of sand. In other words, there was a considerable mahogany cradle dreaming a child's dream.

Remembering the past is preserving the future because the true vengeance of the years is in the spirit's flesh. Because dreams are closest to reality because my name is Sebastián Mortera, I contemplate how the dust on the road plays with the eternal wind beyond the cliff because words define reality; reality is the words themselves because poets perceive words as fish. Because words are fish, and fish swim in ink. That is, when the poet writes, the fish jump out of the ink. And the written word manifests itself. However, one day, the words become microchips between the poet's fingers. And the sea, with all its fish, has hidden in the cyberspace of memory.

A dream can become the shadow of reality. Because the truth is transformed, because it transcends, changes, is edited, virtualized. Because I see myself going through concave and convex spaces, creating little narratives in the wind. Because a story is the closest thing to a poem, José Emilio Pacheco assures us. But I am attracted by the memory of a poem. For example, where is the memory of a grain of sand located? Because a grain of sand is a poem. Where is the memory of the past located? Where is the memory of the future? Because the present is a poem. And if not, why do we discover the cosmos within the past of the universe? I ask: Could it be that from the future I am witnessing my present? And then I no longer doubt. And I believe that in the asymmetry of two poems, a story is hidden. And if so, will there be a memory within the possibility of the passage of the critical size of matter?

At that moment, in response, the voice of three women was heard manifesting:

— In quantum reality, once a matter becomes more significant than a specific decisive size, it spontaneously updates one of its many possibilities.

And in the asymmetry of a second, the cliff continued to cut the waves that raged without rest. The reef assured that Sebastián Mortera was still in a «non» updated existence, but «yes,» in infinite merely potential scenarios. In other words, Sebastián was in that space that defined the possibility at present. In other words,

The void
engenders water and rock
when the voice
becomes blood and body
in the echo of the whole.

That is,
blood transcends
memory,
6ix
7even
3hree
28ight
17teen

π.

Agua *salá*. A nocturnal ejaculation. The sea.

In that enormous house with white walls on the reef, Artemis the —poetess would become pregnant that morning. «Copulation is determined,» Pan thought as he climbed the cliffs

—And what will he be called? —Asked Juventino insistently.
—Sebastián Mortera —she assured undoubtedly, on the waves, the moon.

Artemis, 27, and Juventino, 36, copulated under the moon of May in Dionysus' dream. And time and matter in that instant became 1ne.

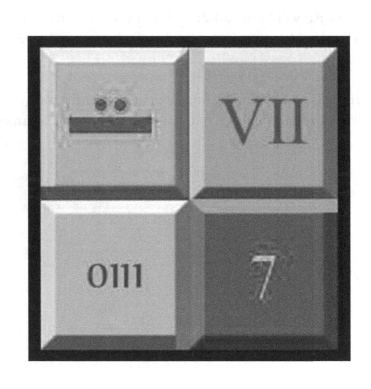

THE TRACE OF THE QUINCUNX

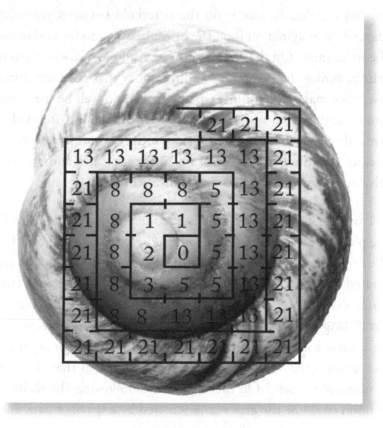

NARRATIVE
© 2002 Edel Romay

NOTE TO THE READER AS A GUIDE

*T*he reality of dreams is found in the quantum reality of memory, or at least, that's my theory. I dream, therefore I am. I remember because I am living. I am because I am remembering. And all this is happening somewhere in my mind.

On the one hand, it is said that our present is located in the space of three seconds; that is, everything else is simply reminiscence or anticipation, past or future. Today, tomorrow will be yesterday. And it strikes me that fantasy is on the threshold between yesterday and today, while imagination is on the brink between today and tomorrow, a theory of mine. On the other hand, the reality we experience is rooted in the yesterday that was today and the today that was once tomorrow. Now, if we make a quantum leap, dreams could well be the product of cosmic memory. I'm not teasing you! Remember: we are made up of cosmic dust, which makes me think that the brain (matter) creates and recreates the mind, and the reason, in turn, creates and recreates the brain; and, therefore, the cosmos—another theory of mine.

I wonder: Is it that dreams lack time and space? Because I don't have proof to the contrary, however, my dreams are so real that I end up believing that they are true. Are they holograms of reality, or are they narrated in a universal language, since, somehow, in dreams, language becomes one? And when this happens, without you being able to avoid it, the imagination decides to look into the mirror only to find the reflection of a language full of symbols, signs, and imaginary incognito. This reminds me of Martin Heidegger, who stated that «Language is the home of the self." On the other hand, following the skein thread, the brain could be the grey matter created by a spark of dark energy.

POINT 0 1 1, OF DEPARTURE...

*I*n those distant days when the gods walked on the Cēmānāhuac, they listened through their eyes, looked through their ears, meditated through their mouths, and the words were almost the exact reflection of what they imagined. The witches assure us that the imagination of the gods was, in truth, what gave rise to the manifestation of humans on earth; everything happened in a cosmic nanosecond. Later, in Cēmānāhuac, a millennial culture witnessed the mouth observing, the eye meditating and the words speaking, which they considered a sign. A symbol that led them to interpret the duality of reality, which they called Ometeotl[12]. And so, it was that Ometeotl initiated the avatar of the gods in the Olmec imagination[13].

The narrative of «The trace of the quincunx[14]» will be woven in the Calmécac as you discover or recreate it. The symbolism will be there, the signs will be there, and you will be there. Of course, the etymology of Calmécac comes from the Nahuatl calli, and means' house,' and mécatl, which means 'rope,' 'string,' or 'cord.' That is, the house of ropes, better known as the house of times. See, you have begun to «weave» since you have associated it with string theory. On the other

---

[12] The word comes from *ome,* which means 'two', and *teotl,* which means 'energy' or 'God', and which explains the name of the principle of duality.

[13] *Olmeca* means 'people from the country of rubber'. It's the name of a mysterious culture, some 5000 years before our era. It flourished in what is now the southeast of the state of Veracruz and the northwest of the state of Tabasco. They were the creators of the jaguar-man.

[14] The original quincunx (according to Universidad Nacional Autónoma de México) is drawn based on a square with an area of 9 units, and each square unit is represented, in turn, by a square. The graph highlights the difference between a group of 4 units and another of 5. It constitutes the starting point of the fractal tolteca series, whose spiral movement repeats to the quincunx in an increasing or decreasing manner, according to the Fibonacci series: 0, 1, 1, 2, 3, 5, 8, 13, 21...

hand, the Olmecs conceptualized their cosmological universe with unprecedented elegance and just three signs.

ZERO	ONE	FIVE
◉	•	▬

CYCLICAL SUCCESSION: (1) (5) (20) (260) (360) = 9360000 days.

Vigesimal years = 9360000 ÷ 360 = 26,000 years.
Vague years = 9360000 ÷ 365 = 25,643.8356 years.
Tropical years = 9360000 ÷ 365,2422 = 25,626.8306 years.
Solar year determined by modern astronomy = 365,242191 days.

DREAM 1 1 2 DREAM

« *T*he flesh, that corporal substance that we carry instinctively on our shoulders, ages, and decays, but it also thinks and remembers» I heard someone look at me in my ear because, ear in hand, I was able to witness the image of Malinche[15]. She came pearled with dew, radiating shades of amber and cocoa; on her thighs, she wore delicate brushstrokes of an ultramarine distance. She sailed on a shield of sacred bird feathers along with lapis lazuli songs and dances. When I felt her approach, a stream of acrylic primary colors began to flow down my chest with such intensity that my temples opened, palpitating like snakes devoured by enormous flint eagles. At that moment, the liquid words of the snake woman (Cihuacóatl) sprouted from the bunch of flowers being carried by an Indian woman in the tianguis ('market'):

---

[15] Malinche, Malinalli ('grass'), Malintzin ('twisted grass') and Marina are the same person. Marina is the Christian name with which this beautiful woman was baptized. Malinche, according to Ricardo Herren, «is a Mexican deformation of Malintzin, applicable to Cortés… however, Malinche is the name with which Marina has gone down in history and popular culture».

The eagle, the *Quilaztli* eagle, the one
painted with snakes' blood, whose crest is made
of eagle feathers, the *Sabino* from those of *Chalma*,
the one from *Colhuacan*[16].

Upon hearing the Nahuatl language in that instant, the tone of her voice echoed between the dream she was dreaming and that magical interval of being almost awake in the penultimate dream. That is, at the end of my first dream, I heard someone shouting, "Aphrodite! Venus! leaving the Calmécac," at the same time that Malinalli was blowing bubbles of marine notes that subtly stimulated my senses. I could notice that she mused a lewd confession to me with a singing voice dyed indigo blue: «Sometimes I think that when I walk naked, the dew of the early morning hides beneath my moss-covered and marine belly.» I felt her through my skin because my eyes scanned her slowly and I saw her gradually mold beneath my deliberate caresses. I listened to her with my eyes in the manner of a woman philosopher who was also a poet. I came slowly, cautiously stalking her steps as if, as she walked, her stealthy movements were made of shade. She arrived with her womanly shapes embracing the ever-narrower space that separated us. The presence was sensual, daring, and innocent; at that precise moment, I invented her, with mute words, I created her. I recreated her like a feral cat that danced to the beat of the notes of the Amazonian music played by Huayucaltía[17]. The mahogany language of her sensuality vibrated intensely under the spell of enchanting melodies emanating from ancestral instruments played gracefully by Indian musicians. The intoxicating rhythm transported me to the most erogenous places of my being when I suddenly realized that my body was morphing into a hummingbird, for I saw myself fluttering vertiginously in search of the soft nectar of the Xochiyotl. And I sank into that sea of petals, feeling my obsidian body shake like a snake devoured by the eagle of the rising

---

[16]   Ángel María Garibay: *Poesía indígena de la Altiplanicie*, 2nd ed., Mexico: Ediciones de la Universidad Nacional Autónoma de México, 1952, p. 15.

[17]   Musical group. The word means 'unity and brotherhood'.

Sun. Then, the fire-colored bird offered me the divine floral color on the left, which I fearlessly took. I, the mushroom taker, radiated yellow, green, blue, red tones as I entered and exited the vertex flower of life. In that flowery communion, I joined the poet of the Jaguar Moon in those times of the Eagle Sun. And that's how I heard her whisper the warrior song to me.

DREAM 1 2 3 DREAM

XOCHIYOTL

Xochiyaoyotl[18], *Xochiyaoyotl*.

Falling is
the red flowers quiveringly touching
the face of the Sun Eagle.

East Sun. West Sun. East Sun.

The end of the beginning
of a drop of blood
for wanting to be a flower.

Wind,
with your gaze of a jet-black bull
Quetzalcoatl[19] returns
on his ship of snakes.

Eagle spins, spins, sunflower
the open petals of the flowers
are singing:

Xochiyaoyotl, Xochiyaoyotl.

---

18 'Flower war' or 'tournament between jaguar warriors (warriors of the night) and Eagle warriors (warriors of the day)'.

19 'Feathered serpent', 'beautiful twin'. Manifestation of the planet Venus, morning star, afternoon star.

DREAM 2 3 5 DREAM

*I*n the clearing of a forest, not far from the shore of a green lagoon flooded with lizards, 4our beings suddenly appeared, mirror in hand, exchanging eyes, tongues, glances, and words. They formed a square, and each occupied a corner. The landscape was radiant, and the colors were intense. I could see that Theophilus is dress in red and that Theodora is dress in blue. In the other two corners, poems were dressing in purple, and philosophy is dress in green. The four wore the same mask designed in leather and clay and Toltec enigmas inscribed on their tongues[20]. There is an islet where Thanatos and Eros played at balancing with a hummingbird, dancing on the red flowers of the cactus. On the same islet, the tree of life outlined a cross, a pyramid, and the circular stone of the divine calendar divided exactly into 20wenty equal segments. At that instant, the day arrived where the night began when the hummingbird god[21] exclaimed: «The sun's journey is sacred.»

Seconds later, the obsidian night split open only to let out a massive stain of fireflies. «Let there be light!» And the light was with me again. The image was clear; the hummingbird god rushed out in search of the floral nectar emanating from the heart of the gentle flower, while the yellow feathers helped the obsidian butterfly take flight. This ritual justified the human sacrifice of which Quetzalcoatl was not a supporter.

«The cosmogonic thought of Anahuac is complex — I thought —, because, inside an empty snail, a blind sea of rattles dances for joy while divine mother Teteoinnan[22] hides in the receptacle partially

---

[20]   Ancient Mexican civilization with the highest degree of spiritual, cultural and technological development (VI to XII centuries) XII).

[21]   According to Yollocalli, it is made up by huitzili, which means 'hummingbird', 'chupamirto', 'chupaflores', and opochtli, which means 'left side'. There is a city associated with this deity that is called Tzintzuntzan, or 'place of the hummingbird god'.

[22]   Mother of the gods.

buried on the beach.» On the beach, a beautiful woman painted in light blue appeared and gently led me to the dimension of an enormous mirror in the shadows, where I saw that the canvas of *The Last Supper* triumphantly penetrated Cem Anahuac. The size of the mirror began to turn into a nightmare when, in the distance, I discovered a sorcerer sitting on a pyramid facing south. I caught him counting tiny planets in the morning dewdrops, and he saw me with his ears and cautiously turned barely to his left to meet your face. And without pronouncing a word, he told me: «Your European mirror face has been painted with almost the same ritual "may this wine be my blood." And do not be scandalized when you witness the same signs and symbols in the ancient archaeology of Cem Anahuac.»

«Here, in this place, death contains both masculine and feminine. As does life itself,» a hummingbird shouted in my right eye, as my left ear saw Mictlantecuhtli-Mictlancíhuatl[23] and Xiuhtecuhtli-Coatlicue play at balancing with a fighting bull over the Greco-Roman waters of the Mediterranean. At that moment, I saw myself coming out of the dimension of the mirror.

---

[23]   Lord and Lady of the Dead.

DREAM 3 5 8 DREAM

I was watching the firefly-crowned jaguar woman playing happily in the sand on the beach. It was dusk, and the shades seemed to intensify their last glow before riding into the dark ultramarine when, suddenly, a jet-black fighting bull appeared from the sea, threatening to ram the beach. At that instant, the jaguar woman turned west in search of the fifth cardinal point, where it was predicted that an eagle, a snake, and a cactus would symbolize the trilogy of a new nation. While this was happening, my tongue was filled with crickets, lizards, rattles, and butterflies, which suddenly flooded my thoughts. Confused, I turned to the left and found myself in front of a clairvoyant sorcerer who told native stories in the Nahuatl language. I do not speak the Nahuatl language; however, the sorcerer guessed my question before even asking him:

—The legend has become real —he said.
Which legend? —I asked.
—La Cruz de Martín —he answered.

I stared at him even more confused, since I had understood his language, and, without opening his mouth, he continued:

—The tattooed tongues of Olmec incognitos had predicted that Malinche would wait for either of the lovers to impregnate her. And so, it was that a drop of blood named Martin left for Spain to return to Mexico as «the first Mexican,» according to Carlos Fuentes. On the other hand, the Christian religion put down deep roots in this land.

I was about to ask him about Marina's other lover when I was suddenly transported to another dimension within the same Calmécac. This appearing and disappearing in more than two places at once made me ponder on string theory. That is to say, and I was simultaneously driven into and out of the shaded mural that reflected two parallel dimensions. In one was the poet-painter, mixing blue with red and creating an image filled with cactus thorns while the earth rested on the head of a giant lizard. The painter-philosopher was the other dimension, mixing green with yellow and creating an echo in Olmec architecture. Then the tree of life was reflected in the lake's mirror, and it led me to the thirteenth sky, better known as Omeyocan[24].

The count began with zero, from creating the first Sun to the culmination of this fifth Sun. On December 21, 2012, the Fifth Sun died of our era, which accounts for 25, 626.8306 years. That's right! The Fifth Sun began on August 13, 3113.18306 B.C. See! Add this to the previous amount 2012.18306, and you get 5125.36612 years, which is the duration of a sun. The sum of the five suns makes an era of 25,626.8306 years. This picture is the fabric that they left us. And you are already associating it with string theory. And you're right, even though it sounds a little esoteric.

---

[24] Universe, place where duality occurs.

DREAM 5 8 13 DREAM

I was contemplating the threads of fabric showing me a design intertwined by the melodious voice of a beautiful indigenous woman when I realized that the language in which she expressed herself was not my own. Yet, I could understand what she was saying:

"Xochincuahuitl, or Flowering Tree, broke off a quetzal heading south;
»a jaguar heading east;
»an eagle heading north;
»a hummingbird is heading west.
»In the center, Cipactli[25].

»Then, from the imagination of a beetle, four serpents manifested, which, in truth, were only one woman. From this woman's imagination, four butterflies were displayed, only one flower (Xochitl). From the vision of Xochitl, five amphoras manifested, which, in truth, were a single jar of water. From the mouth of this pitcher, the mother of the gods extracted the Mexican woman.

"In that instant, the Pyramid of the Sun manifested; where 2wo jaguars and 3hree eagles talked very vivaciously:
»— Malinalli is a young eagle that senses in her heart the sharpness of a bullfighting thrust produced by a spine of maguey —said eagle one (south).
»— Malintzin is a jaguar that adopts languages. His beautiful eyes, like fish, devour words. He listens by his sight that enormous horses come mounted by men dressed in steel and that spew fire —explained jaguar one (west).

---

25 *Cipactli* means 'lizard, 'caiman'. Enormous reptile that carries the Earth over spring waters. It also represents the first day and the number zero.

»— Every morning, a beautiful Mexican girl narrates the fierce brawl still held by Quetzalcoatl and Tezcatlipoca[26]. On the shore of the gulf, there are traces of Indian dances, and, from the port, shadows are pointing to Europe —added eagle two (east).

»— Marina is the magical-oneiric image in the voice of Mexican poet Agustín Lara when he sings *Veracruz* or *Granada*... —expressed jaguar two (north).

»— A tropical woman of wind, dust, and legend rises above herself and then crashes into a steel armor that eats wheat bread, drinks grape blood, and prays a Hail Mary in the name of a sacred heart painted on its chest —finalized eagle three (center).»

I was trying to understand the symbology of this painting when, suddenly, I was transported to my penultimate dream. I resisted, but it was pointless. Another voice was calling me.

---

[26]   Deity of the night. The word means 'black obsidian mirror'.

Pause: 13teen seconds before waking

I was driven through ghostly spaces by a sensual woman with the aroma of guava, mango, and ripe soursop. The scent of fruit, believe me, ran lightly through her breasts that floated undecided between my fingers. Then I noticed a gentle sun frolicking over a peach-colored sky and a bull wind filling itself with beetles. The bull wind, when it felt observed, gently blew the wet sex of the young Malintzin. She let out a groan of joy as she placed my Minotaur face between her round breasts. We both fell into a soft abandonment of caresses until the dusk, with its dance of mosquitoes landing voraciously on the coconut palms. The taurine shade of the night fell carelessly on our naked bodies as the beach ran behind the elusive sea. Just then, I realized that it was part of a painting, of cloth, of a fabric. And that, in the same way, the sea breeze was freshly applied oil paint. However, on the other side of the painting, the evening mist seemed to stimulate the sorcerer painter to identify two bodies illuminated and eroticized by fire beetles between the mountain and the sea. The sorcerer painter looked at his work, took a still wet paint brush, and drew an enfolding embrace of two shadows that joined. And so he continued to bring the two naked bodies, which were intensely filled by the night, the beach and the spell, closer together with the force of brilliant brushstrokes. At that very moment, on the other side of the dream, the bunch of flowers carried by an Indian woman in the market resounded the liquid words of the feathered Minotaur with snake horns: «Memory is hidden in the word, and words are hidden in the imagination.» Just then, the imagination proceeded to mix poetry with science, and vice versa, and left on the beach a snail half sunk in the sand, memorizing the natural cadence that the sea was forming in the air.

The interval between being asleep and being awake is that feeling of knowing that you are occupying two dimensions simultaneously. Despite knowing it is tough to do, it is that delicious and attractive mixture of wanting to continue the same dream. But you keep trying in vain. «There is no point —I tell you—, you are awake already!». Am I awake?

POINT OF ARRIVAL

«What a dream!» I said to myself, for I woke up a little lost. I thought I was in the port of Veracruz, but I was still stationed in the 21st century, living in the city of Barcelona. I could have sworn that I was in another space and at another time. The experience was so real that I panicked irrationally. To my delight, a beautiful Catalan girl lay lovingly on my bed, with that Mediterranean *je ne sais quoi*. There was no doubt I was at home; the woman in my dream also had a *je ne sais quoi* proper to the Gulf of Mexico. « In the dream, both women are the same and neither at the same time —I told myself—. The reality of the dream lies in another dimension. Perhaps, in the duality of the mirror or in the diversity of reflection, who knows!» these are the lucubrations I was in when Mariella woke up and kissed me on the cheek.

— You haven't asked me about the six guitars —I said timidly.
— The strings? —she asked, undecided.
— Of course! The strings —I hurried to answer.
— Do you mean the threads we've been weaving the trace of the quincunx with?
—Probably—I answered.

POINT OF DEPARTURE...

«I'm here, the other, the one who's watching you on the other side of this reality,» you flirted with me while, naked, you ran to make a cup of coffee in the kitchen. I was left somewhat meditative and conversing with myself: «Am I dreaming?... Of course not! I'm sure I am awake, either in this dimension or the other... But what matters is that she is here».

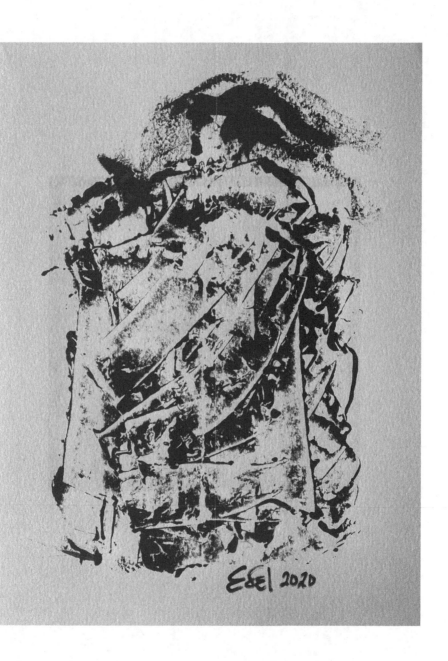

Edel 2020

THE FOREST IN A SINGLE TREE

Narrative
©2002 Edel Romay

PROLOGUE

*B*efore disappearing, the tree weeps for your immediate future extinction because without it; there is no you; without you, there is no me. And the cosmos will not notice the human's absence even for an instant.

—In whose mind will the last observation remain? —She asks, —he asks, —you ask.

And I straightaway answer them:

—I have no idea; however, the tree, before becoming the paper I am writing on, provided us with oxygen, shelter, sustenance, shade, and company, at the very least. Then, already as paper, it evolved into a book. And the book, in turn, became your inseparable friend. However, after centuries of being your best advisor, now, at this instant, you are calling it a traditional book; in other words, it is beginning to disappear. Twenty-first-century technology is making it digital. And we, like the conventional book, are following suit; the same technology is taking us through a logical process of transformation.

On the one hand, most know that organic life, including that of the human being, is based on carbon-12 and that human reality is only understood with human observation. On the other hand, technology has advanced by leaps and bounds at the beginning of the 21st century, making me think that Human-like entities of our creation will gradually replace us, Humans. And if this were to happen, the beings of that immediate reality could well reduce human history to a simple myth. It is plausible; our prehistory has been reduced to tales. For example, today, we study Greek, Egyptian, Mesopotamian, and Roman mythology. However, little or nothing is known about the mythology of the Cēm Ānāhuac.

The grandmother's forest, 1948

*T*he leaves seemed to fall to the bottom of the forest with no memory of having been a fundamental part of the tree branches. «The Forest in a Single Tree,» thought the seed, and the naked stems continued to ignore that the leaves had been part of them. «The memory of the wind,» the roots reflected. «The subsoil of sleep,» the restless insects meditated.

Vertically, above, the leaves may well have rubbed together sensually in the wind. Perhaps they even imitated birds in flight. Or they may have turned into sunglasses one day. Or in full moon cups for some magical nights. Maybe they even played musicals in the rain and later became the *Danzón* of nocturnal insects. However, in the memory of the memory, let it be evident! Neighbor to the roots, horizontally, below, was sepia dampness, carpet for my steps, shelter for another small world.

After three years on the hacienda, Grandma's yard was a little small for the precocious imagination of a nine-year-old boy who believed that the Earth was a grain of sand. And if I remember correctly one day, something unusual happened: the courtyard grew in the forest until it reached the cosmic dimensions of the jungle, and I dare to venture that it was for the sole purpose of accommodating the imagination of children. At the very least, those of us who believed that trees were living beings and that they were disguised with stems and foliage only to mislead us.

At that time, it was 1948, but for my cousins, my brother, and me, time seemed to be in no hurry. A week till Sunday, immeasurable. A Thursday of waiting for the Cine Lux function, inconceivable. A year until Three Kings Day, infinite. The time of the «elders» was conceived only by pretending that we believed it to be true. Yesterday was «I don't remember.» Tomorrow did not exist; that is to say, reality covered only that present moment, that precise space of today where the real world of children manifested itself. However, attending the Freinet School of Patricio Redondo Moreno, a republican Spaniard exiled to Mexican lands, was to conjugate the times of adults with our times. There existed reality and imagination simultaneously. The tools were linen and gouges, engraving, paper, and printing with which we produced the Xóchitl magazine. At the Freinet School, imagination accompanied me to draw and write stories about the birds that knew how to converse with the trees, and I also transcribed the anecdotes that the trees themselves used to tell me. Being parked in the same place in no way limits them. Have you seen how majestic they rise to the sky? They can converse freely with the wind, the sun, the rain, and the night. Ah, in the dark, the trees play with the nocturnal animals at running without being seen!

For four years, my cousins, my brother, and I were expert illusionists in my grandmother's courtyard now turned into a jungle. Mirage makers. We were characters from that imaginary world where fantasy and reality seem to be intimately linked to the game of simulation. In other words, we were polyform actors in work in progress. One day I could be a hunter or just an adventurer in the jungle. Another day, perhaps, pretender of explorer or researcher of the forests. The interpretations were infinite; no doubt, that was the marvelous age where the power of truth was in the imagination of fantasy. There the dialogued monologue was given in the creation of fictitious characters that interacted with us. The sources of inspiration for children's vision can be many and varied. For me, they were my grandfather's library books. And, of course, the radio with its radio stories of suspense and adventures. Cinematography, however, was the best hallucinogen. First, I started with the silent Charlie Chaplin films at the Freinet School; then, with the movie premiering at Cine Lux: Tarzan or Jim of the jungle starring Johnny Weissmüller. How can we forget Tarzan!? How can we forget Jim of the jungle!? If I owned a forest in Grandmother Dolores' courtyard.

Time flies say the old men

*A*nd then, one day, the first signs of puberty appear the first nocturnal ejaculation, a mixture of pleasure, surprise, and apprehension. It is clear: to hide this new condition from others because the indiscreet wet white sheets become a very embarrassing problem in the mornings. My new ritual was to cross my fingers and pray that the «maid» would not go gossiping to my grandmother; everyone would think I had peed in the bed. And it would be embarrassing to explain! Fortunately, no one knew anything. Or, if they noticed, they said nothing. What a relief! But my fantasies had taken a new turn.

I did not find the games I used to play so entertainingly. I was easily bored. I felt that sex was haunting me everywhere. I dreamt or thought I dreamt of having sex with an imaginary woman (the sensuality of Ninón Sevilla made me horny), and making love to her was so real that I found myself wet when I woke up with that egg white-like viscous liquid. I stroked my sex, and it looked like a nervous fish trying to escape my hand. We made love so many times in my imagination that I could no longer remember where or when. Ever since I saw her in the cinema, I fell in love with her; and how could I not fall in love with her when she was so pretty and sensual!

On the other hand, I think I fell romantically in love with Clementina, and Lydia, and Selma, because I was writing poems that I recited alone because, for some reason, I did not dare even read them to the women. The truth is that I did not know what was happening to me: I liked solitude, and, suddenly, I was talking to myself. At other times I decided to engrave their names with the mountain knife on the thick trunks of the trees that once spoke to me, perhaps seeking advice. Or I would read my poems aloud to them to see what they would say, but it seemed that the trees had been left speechless. It was apparent that they refused to talk to me. They spoke only with the wind; I could hear them because I heard the rustling of the foliage, but I no longer understood the tone of their language.

The senses no longer responded to the same stimuli. Sensuality haunted me everywhere, and my older cousins were to blame, for they were the ones who encouraged me to play delightfully lascivious mischief with the maids. And I accepted the challenge! Of course, that original game induced me to discover a new language. And I was shyly led by that beautiful girl who provocatively laughed as she undressed me with her hands until she touched the erection of my passion. And so, little by little, the caresses became more daring until I caressed round breasts and hard nipples with my lips. Then I kissed her wet lips and, without thinking about it, I plunged into her sex. I closed my eyes and let myself be carried away by a series of new and exquisite sensations. The feast had no measure since, in a short time, those young girls taught me the ecstasy of full sex.

Everyday reality can change overnight. It happened to me, suddenly, without me being able to avoid it. At dawn, before my eyes, the forest ceased to be a forest and became a courtyard. The avocado seed in the glass of water that had been in my room for weeks finally put down roots and stems. And one day, the branch shouted: «Soon, I'll be the forest in a tree!» Then I hurried and transplanted it into the garden. There it would be surrounded by the eighteen trees that witnessed my intimate world. That little one would stand there full of my fantasies of yesteryear. I had stopped being a child. The first year of high school passed successfully. In that time, the days began to fly; it was the year 1952.

(In brackets), 1992

*F*ive hundred years ago, on October 12, 1492, Spain had reached what was later called America. Do not doubt it! I am referring specifically to the continent. But I clarify, Spain did not set foot in a new world; this world was as old as the world from which the Spaniards came. What is an irrefutable fact is that they conquered at least two-thirds of the continent. I agree! They arrived in boats made of wood, for which they must have cut down a lot of forests. So did the rest of Europe and Asia. And even today, for different reasons, forests continue to be plundered.

Absurd Realism

A bad dream usually ends up being a dreadful nightmare. And most of my dreams have become spooky nightmares. I am apprehensive about the planet's current situation; its environmental predation has reached the most alarming rates. We cannot and must not allow the Earth to become an excellent rubbish dump. Scenes of massive pollution are disturbing, but very few seem concerned about this current reality. What is more, logging, almost everywhere in the world, is on the rise. What an eloquent incredible realism it is to attack the lungs of the world!

Nightmare

«What ignorance! —I exclaimed, irritated— carbon-12 is the basis of organic life,» and I saw myself running along endless paths to a forest. «They are living beings,» I shouted in anguish. But the mechanical monsters kept attacking the trees. And I cried again: «it is the forest that turns carbon dioxide into oxygen!» And the sun, immutable, spun past. The anguish suffocated me when, suddenly, with my last breath, I cried out in rage, «Stop, murderers!»

I woke up sweating and with my heart pounding out of my chest. «It was a frightful nightmare; nevertheless, humans are mowing down trees from the face of the planet,» I said to myself as I tried to fall asleep again.

«The mass media has chosen to «entertain» rather than educate. The discourse is clear: many monetary benefits are to be had from ignorance; the viewers take no action and allow the media to be their eyes and minds, creating a total alienation among the population. It is enough to watch the news programs on T.V. to see how the *Ignoramus Erectus* multiply and express, with clear stupidity, their ignorance about the planet's alarming situation». I saw myself trying to argue with them uselessly, and the more I tried to put forward logical reasoning, the more trivialized or demonized it was. They did not want an intelligent conversation. My anguish was increasing when, suddenly, I thought I heard the tango *Cambalache* from afar in the voice of Tita Merello, and it was then that I was transported to the clearing of a chimerical forest. «There is no doubt about it; this is a nightmare,» he repeated. The stage on which I found myself was a legendary forest stored in the memory of the last observer. The hallucinogenic colors were intermingled in an aphrodisiac dance where the present and the future pointed towards the very absence of the forest itself.

(In brackets), nature reveals itself

In the clearing of a forest, humans, immutably arrogant, formed a closed, concentric circle to indicate that they were there and represented only the human interests of the continent. However, at the center of that circle, a mute parrot executed dialogical arguments in the languages of power. My eyes refused to give credit to what they were witnessing, for I understood the language of animals perfectly. And it was then, at that very moment, that I perceived the animals as being more human than the humans themselves. I realized that man had not understood that he belonged to the animal kingdom, even though it had been proven that he shared the same DNA. Despite this, man still believed that his ancestry was divine. «We all somehow wear the same chemical garb,» I heard them say. However, the people gathered there continued to remain silent and ignored my argument. Come! Let me describe the scene: the forest was drawn in the green waters of a mirror. The spectacle was conceptually preposterous-realistic. See? Little frogs and toads worldwide pointed out that human stupidity refused to accept its suicidal tendency with full knowledge of the facts.

— YES! —They shouted—, every human action leads us to think that they are suicidal: not only has it created holes all over the planet to look for minerals and oil, but now it has also created a sovereign hole in the southern roof of «our home.»

And the humans kept an impervious silence.

— This is an ecological board—added the amphibians—. The ozone layer is being dangerously affected.

And that is when I found out that I understood the supporting dialectic.

—This massive global pollution is a human product — said the polyglot parrot.

—The sea is poisoned — the whale shark intervened emphatically.

—Humans believe they are NOT part of the Earth ecosystem — interrupted the toucan.

—Wow, we share the same DNA —added the frog, the rat, and the chimpanzee.

—There are 5743 species of amphibians known to humans — added the harlequin frog.

—A third is about to disappear! —You shouted.

— Humans are suicidal! —Exclaimed all the amphibians of the planet.

—The degradation of the habitat is the work of man —concluded the frogs.

—Massive global pollution affects everyone the same! —Cried flora and fauna in a rage.

December 21, 2012

*T*rying to capture time has undoubtedly been a human task since Humans became aware that they had memory, that they could remember, count, measure, draw, write; in other words, they could keep a record and save an event. A process that somehow freed them from the constraint of nostalgia for the fleeting present. Traces of this are to be found in history, which is the collective memory of humanity. Let us look at an example. In 45 B.C., Julius Caesar implanted the Julian calendar, which was in force until the Renaissance. In 1582, the Julian calendar was replaced by the Gregorian calendar in honor of Pope Gregory XIII. The reason for the substitution was that the previous calendar presented certain anomalies in the long count. Thus, the Gregorian calendar corrected these inaccuracies and established 365 days, 5 hours, 48 minutes, and 54 seconds. At present, astronomy has determined that a year lasts 365,24219 days. The figure below describes the chronological line of "before" and "after" Christ is measured. Historical time divided into years, decades, centuries, or millennia is usually expressed by abbreviations a. C or d. C, as corresponds to one or another period.

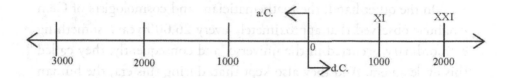

The Cēm Ānāhuac

*T*he Olmecs, Toltecs, Mayans, and Aztecs, among others, established their calendars, incidentally, with surprising accuracy. The fifth sun, with which we are most familiar, is from the Aztec calendar; however, the time count comes from the Olmecs.

According to the prediction, both the "era" and the "age of the fifth sun" concurred at zero on December 21, 2012. Now, I ask: how did you come to this conclusion? Simply put, the ancient sages of Cēm Ānāhuac interpreted the events of the cosmos as the sum of cyclical events. And they conceptualized these events observing that the days were 1 in 1, 5 in 5, 20 in 20, 260 in 260, and 360 in 360. That is, there was a mathematical recurrence such that (1) (5) (20) (260) (360) yielded a sum of nine million three hundred and sixty thousand days (9360000).

The mathematical system in Cēm Ānāhuac was vigesimal. They established the astrological calendar of 260 days, divided into 20 months of 13 days per month. Parallel to this calendar, they created the solar calendar, composed of 360 + 5 days, divided into 18 months of 20 days each; the remaining five days were abstinence. The count began with the number zero. The zero of the calendar of 260 days and the zero-day of (360 + 5) started simultaneously and did not coincide again in 0 until 52 years later. Please take note that the number 0, it seems, enjoyed considerable importance in the Cēm Ānāhuac, since to identify it, they used several symbols, some of which are difficult for me to describe; others, in contrast, are obvious: faces, half a flower, or a snail.

On the other hand, the mathematicians and cosmologists of Cēm Ānāhuac observed that approximately every 26,000 years, something extraordinary occurred in the universe, and consequently, they called this cycle an era. And they also kept that, during this era, the human being went through 5 ages of transformation. To follow its logic: the long count is composed of 9360000 and, dividing it by the twentieth year, it gives us 26000 round years. We divide 26000 years by five and get 5200 years. This progression is articulated as follows:

The first age or first sun was called: Water Sun.

The second age or second sun was given the name: Feline Sun.

The third age or third sun was named: Rain of Fire.

The fourth age or fourth sun was called: Sun of Storms.

The fifth age or Fifth Sun was attributed the name: Sun of the Movement.

According to Cēm Ānāhuac, the era and the fifth age ended on December 21, 2012. I will try to explain how they came to this conclusion. In Cēm Ānāhuac, several other calendars were handled in parallel, for example, the one of (364 + 1), which gives the impression that it indicated the seasons of the year, among other things, since the pyramid to Kukulcan is designed in such a way that on each side there are 91 steps plus the last one in the cusp, that is [(91 x 4 = 364) + 1]. The other calendar was the tropical year, calculated, to our astonishment, at 365,2422 days. This calendar is handled in real-time. Going deeper, we find that the age of this era in real-time is found by dividing the long count of 9360000 by the tropical year of 365.2422, which yields the amount of 25626.8306 years. If we divide this amount by five, it gives us 5125.36612 years. See! Impressive: first sun, 5125.36612 years; second sun, 5125.36612 years; third sun, 5125.36612 years; fourth sun, 5125.36612 years; and Fifth Sun, 5125.36612 years.

Extrapolating the reasoning behind the Cēm Ānāhuac to the Gregorian calendar to understand it, we find that the fourth sun ended on December 21, 3113 B.C. at midnight. And, immediately, on December 22, 3113 B.C., the count of the Fifth Sun, also 5125.36612 years old, began. Is that clear? Add 3113.18306 to 2012.18306, and you will get the exact age of the fifth, of 5125.36612 years. And that's how one era came to an end, and another era, of 25626.8306, began on December 22, 2012. I agree! I will put the age of the Fifth Sun in parallel with the Gregorian calendar to see the correlation of historical time. Let's look at the figure:

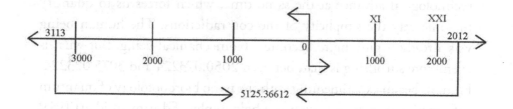

Wait a minute, don't get confused; the sixth sun didn't start. Remember the scientific philosophy of the Cēm Ānāhuac, which emphasizes that every event in the universe is cyclical. Thus, the sixth sun did not begin, but the era (25626,8306 years) began with Soluno on December 22, 2012.

Soluno: quantum leap, the year 4100.073224

«*A*ttention —said the quantum cybernetic professor—, we have established that 2012 of the Gregorian calendars is zero so that Soluno started from that moment. This leads us to analyze a before and an after of these zero origins. For example, we designate the period from 1000 to 2012 of the Gregorian calendars as *prehistoric*. After 2012, *a new era*. I will project the following graph:

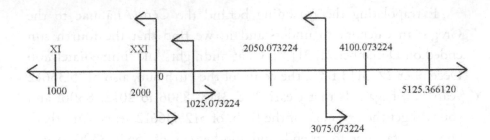

During Soluno's first 1025.073224 years, forests and jungles gradually began to disappear from the planet. However, between 1025.073224 and 2050. 073224 there was a surprising and contradictory scientific-technological advance at the same time, which forces us to quantify in some way the simplicity of the contradictions. The human being was already beginning to become a biomechanical being. But what is even more surprising is that, between 2050.073224 and 3075.073224, humans began experimenting with the nano biorobotology of quantum information of memory, quantum holography of dreams, and artificial quantum intelligence. And, at a given moment, it was creating, in its likeness, other beings that, in turn, created other beings that, in turn, created other new beings. And it is not known precisely when cybernetic quantum information began a new reality where the quantum consciousness of the mind of artificial intelligence was intertwined with the human mind, at least, as what was then defined as human. And so, later, the human became history, and then prehistory, until he became a myth of a derisory reality stored in the information of a few isolated quantum microchips to define something known. However, luckily for us, the memory of quantum artificial intelligence kept «something» of what could have been human existence as such.

Megalithic archaeology of memory

*D*espite the difficulty, a minimal amount of substantive information could be rescued. The translation into our language has been highly creative, as we have had to extrapolate the content to be understood as somehow logical. Two readings were processed:

Reading A

Fixing some space-time in history, we could assure that yesterday, all the jungles and forests were manifested as a torrential downpour in the immensity of the imagination of planet Earth. And planetoid dreams of a trillion trillion beings dwelled in those magical places. From the outer scrutiny of an astronaut, some time ago, the jungles and forests seemed to hide invisibly in the celestial roundness of the world. Today, the planet gravitates like a grain of sand in the immensity of the cosmos.

Reading B

For Chico Mendes, the forest and other, almost infinite, ecosystems were as humid, tender, and warm as a tropical woman's sex. Planetoids dream of Chico Mendes and of a trillion entities that, without a logical reason, were assassinated by the symbolic deft of the ax. The forests and jungles were systematically reduced. Like Chico Mendes, all the trees on the planet continued to fall daily. Now, the beautiful goddess of at least 3.5 billion years (Gaia) has no trace on the skin of her ancient forests and jungles.

Current date: Soluno, 4100.073224 years

«*E*ra 2, Soluno, 4100.073224», and he repeated the date as if to make sure that they had understood the importance of the present historical time in comparison to the historical time of the human. He then connected to the student cyber network: «This date marks a very significant event. Of the few vestiges that were saved from the "human memory," a most unusual and illogical finding was discovered, that is to say, what they called life was supported by carbon-12. But it has been proven, without a doubt, that the carbon-12 for our existence is completely unstable, fatal. The study of mythology as such is entertaining; however, human mythology is just that: mythology!» The quantum cybernetic professor ended by telling the audience, 1025.292896 years before Soluno reached zero counts on December 21, 5125.36612.

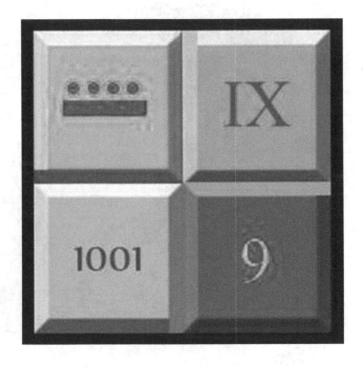

THE RELATIVITY OF THE VERY LARGE

Narrative
© 2007 Edel Romay

WATCH OUT FOR SIZES
AND PROPORTIONS

I was a very perceptive boy, dedicated to looking and asking. So, it soon dawned on me that objects of different sizes coexisted in the world around me. And that the meter was the Standard of measure. If I remember correctly, I was in the third grade of primary school. One day, when I was running, I fell and scraped my knees. My cousin who was in high school laughed and said:

—Gravity is to blame.
—And what is gravity? —I asked him.
—It is the force of attraction of the Earth —he answered flatly.

On another occasion, Esther, the doctor who was staying at our house and doing her social service, explained that the device she was cleaning was called a microscope and that with it, I could see what I could not see with the naked eye. She also explained that another device pointed to the stars, and that was called a *telescope*.

—What is the telescope for? — I asked her.
—To see what you can not see with the naked eye —she replied.
—I do not understand —I said.
—You see, the stars seem very small because they are very far away from us, but they are gigantic compared to our star that we call *Sun*. Besides, some stars cannot be seen with the naked eye because they are even more distant from the Earth.

Esther was a beautiful girl with inquisitive green eyes. After this explanation, I began to think: «I exist between the enormously large and the tremendously small. In other words, between the telescope and the microscope. I live in that space that separates the infinitely small from the infinitely large, which we have agreed to call reality. However, neither dimension can be seen with the naked eye, but they both still exist. On one end is the nano reality of the infinitely small, and on the other end, the immeasurable REALITY of the universe. Over the years, I conceived it as [REALITY (Reality) reality].

Before 1972

*D*on Evaristo Epigmenio Sotomayor Rubalcaba was an intelligent man, corpulent and a bit rough in his social dealings, but he «had a heart of gold,» the locals used to say. His ancestry dates back to the 19ᵗʰ century. Don Evaristo, from his name, is easy to guess; he came from a wealthy, old family, primarily dedicated to cattle ranching. Both the Sotomayor and the Rubalcaba families had amassed their fortune because they owned large tracts of land. Sotomayor and Rubalcaba arrived in the spring of 1800 by special invitation of the then heir to the Marquisate, the Count of Terranova and Duke of Monteleone. They settled in what is now known as Las Higueras.

Las Higueras

By 1823, the Sotomayor's owned about 70 sites (130,000 hectares), approximately 40,000 cattle, and about 5,000 horses. Raised cattle and monopolized the Butchers shops in town. The Rubalcaba's owned 32 sites (58,000 hectares). The Rubalcaba's trade seeds and held all the grocery stores in town. The Sotomayor had dominated the municipal presidency, and the Rubalcaba had remained in the courthouse and the Civil Registry. Of course, despite having almost everything, they were no strangers to misfortune: over the years, they had lost their loved ones, either because of cholera that struck the region in the early decades of the nineteenth century or through the armed uprisings, especially at the beginning of the twentieth century. If that weren't enough, there were also the occasional quarrels between the youth due to passionate loves, natural phenomena, or unforeseen accidents. The truth is that losing a loved one has no cure.

Don Evaristo lost his wife and two daughters in 1962 when they were leaving San Andrés Tuxtla for Catemaco, in that dangerous curve witness to so many tragedies.

After 1972

Eugenio Leopoldo Sotomayor Fernández lost his parents in 1974, at the age of 2, when his father, Leopoldo Alberto Sotomayor Rubalcaba, don Evaristo's younger brother, was driving his brand-new car, a Ford Galaxy 500, 1974. Miraculously, the boy was the only survivor of such a dramatic accident. When people ran to help, they found him sitting a few meters away from the highway, playing with a few pebbles. The car had fallen into the ravine and caught fire. «It wasn't his time to go to God,» said the good people of the town. And, as a rooster crowed, they went to tell Don Evaristo what had happened.

Synopsis

Los Tuxtlas is an atavistic, seductive, and enigmatic setting for forests, rivers, waterfalls, and lakes. A conclave in which history, myth, legend, tradition, magic, and modernity are interwoven. In this region, we can go back to the Olmec culture. Like faithful sentinels, the colossal heads, the architecture, the sculptures, and the ceramics tell us today about their traditions, myths, and legends. For example, in the Totonaca, Popoluca, and Nahuatl languages, you can see the bird's kingdom converge with that of the serpent (Quetzalcoatl).

On the other hand, the forest preserves the metamorphosis of the jaguar woman. That said, the region maintained a strong resistance against the Aztec Empire. And the Spanish Empire somehow perceived the Achilles heel of the Aztecs after having penetrated the Cēm Ānāhuac. Later, the Spaniards added the worldview of the Africans, brought as a labor force to the sugar mills. As time went by, other smaller groups added more cultural wealth to what is now known as the Los Tuxtlas region. This linguistic-cultural amalgam was also interweaving an esoteric mantle where the supernatural coincides, in a given moment, with the real and with the dreamlike, in other words, witchcraft. And witchcraft is a common practice throughout the area.

(In brackets)

Stories abound here, and it is said that Eugenio's mother, Mrs. Victoria Ángela Fernández Huerta, was attended by a *curandera* and a sorcerer at the hacienda on March 1, 1972, when her labor pains began afternoon. Neither the driver nor the truck was at the hacienda, so the closest help was Doña Julia and Teófilo. Fortunately, there were no complications. Leopoldo Alberto Sotomayor Rubalcaba arrived in the afternoon and was pleasantly surprised to find a baby boy with big expressive eyes. Vitoria Ángela was in charge of telling him the details; for example, she said to him that both the curandera and the sorcerer had predicted good omens for Eugenio. Doña Julia and Teófilo agreed that the child had been born with the gift of sorcery and that he was a seer. Leopold Albert only shook his condescending head with what Victoria Angela told him with so much ado.

Eugenio Leopoldo Sotomayor Fernández

He was a child of the thin constitution and fragile health. From a very early age, he showed signs of being very intelligent. He learned to read before speaking, and when Eugenio began to talk, he never stopped. However, his world was made up of books and the contemplation of starry nights. And Don Evaristo was always there, as a father, mother, and friend, trying to answer the many questions that Eugenio asked him. He was always the first in elementary school and graduated with honors; this was also true for high school, where his favorite classes were math and physics. «A child prodigy,» his teachers used to say.

Proud of his nephew's achievements, Don Evaristo sent him to Universidad Veracruzana to study what he thought was a profitable career. In Xalapa, while he was in Preparatory school, he was not convinced of choosing engineering, philosophy, or medicine simply because he liked mathematics more. He had a knack for formulas and their abstract content, which stimulated his imagination. So, he did not hesitate to devote himself entirely to the study of pure mathematics. However, when he finally graduated from high school, awarded for having reached the highest grades, he did not tell Don Evaristo what his actual decision had been. Still, at a given moment, between the joy and happiness of both, he asked him the following question:

—I bet you can't guess which one I've decided on?
—Medicine —answered don Evaristo hugging him.

And nothing more was said. The graduation party took its course while Don Evaristo was left with Eugenio's idea to study medicine. In addition, he was going to go to Universidad Nacional Autónoma de México (UNAM), no less.

As soon as he was in college, he devoted himself to mathematics, and, as was to be expected, he averaged the first grade every year. The uncle trusted his nephew completely, so when he told him that he was going to the United States with a scholarship, Don Evaristo could not have been happier. He shouted to the four winds in the village: "My Eugenio has become a doctor." The truth was different, but he firmly believed that his nephew was studying medicine, which he thought was true. And he imagined that Eugenio was going to specialize, perhaps, in neurology. Admittedly, Don Evaristo had always been given to imagine things beyond the factual. For example, when Eugenio was twenty years old and Anna Victoria was nineteen, Don Evaristo accidentally saw them kiss passionately in the hallway at the entrance to the house and then in the backyard, where the big outdoor parties were usually held. So, he came to the idea that somehow Anna and Eugenio would get married.

Reflexive pause

Curiously, Anna Victoria Rubalcaba Espíndola was born on March 1, 1973, similar to Eugenio's. The van and the driver were out of the hacienda. Mrs. Alma Eduviges Espíndola Oropesa began to have labor pains. They immediately called Mrs. Julia and Don Teófilo, who took care of her quickly. With no difficulty, she gave birth to a pretty girl, who was ritualized by the healer and the sorcerer like Eugenio. Both agreed that the girl would become a healer.

UNAM

Years passed and Mrs. Alma Eduviges Espíndola, with the consent of Mr. Alejandro Francisco Rubalcaba Arguelles, sent her daughter Anna Victoria to study in Mexico City, where her sister lived. Remarkably, Anna Victoria Rubalcaba Espíndola and Eugenio Leopoldo Sotomayor Fernández, from a very young age, kept a close bond, to such an extent that they were seen together all the time. They even entered Universidad Nacional Autónoma de México (UNAM) together, and from where Anna Victoria graduated as a doctor with a specialization in tropical diseases. In the meantime, Anna Victoria and Eugenio Leopoldo had an intense love affair. And even though he went to the United States in 1998, Anna Victoria continued the relationship; so, Eugenio traveled to Mexico City four to five times a year. And in a fated slip, in mid-1999, she became pregnant. However, Anna Victoria did not want to marry Eugenio Leopoldo; of course, Anna Victoria would have the child but would not stay with him. She was not willing to truncate her career and become a mother. And she wasn't born with the gift to be one. She wanted and preferred to dedicate herself totally to her vocation. Anna Victoria graduated as a doctor and was doing her social service. And anyway, neither Eugenio Leopold nor she was in love with each other, and he already had a formal girlfriend: Dianne Odenwald.

Eugenio Leopoldo tried to convince Anna Victoria and finally understood her position. «There are women who don't have that maternal urge,» he said to himself, and so he kept the child. That child, Evaristo Eugenio, was his salvation and that of his girlfriend, who could not have children. Dianne believed everything Eugenio Leopoldo told her: Anna Victoria got pregnant with the boy she was seeing. And as soon as he found out she was pregnant, he left her. Anna's parents were rigorous, and the «what would the neighbors say» would have killed them. Dianne accepted that the child's mother and Anna Victoria agreed: that would be the big secret that the three of them would keep. For Dianne, it was a miracle fallen from the sky; at last, she was going to be a mother. For Anna Victoria, a huge relief, being a mother was not on her agenda.

Eugenio's return

Years passed, I don't know, maybe more than seven, when Eugenio returned to the village in 2007 at 35. He was going to have a well-deserved long vacation. To the amazement of everyone in Las Higueras, Eugenio arrived accompanied by his wife and son. The surprise left Don Evaristo speechless, even more so because the boy had an unmistakable resemblance to him when he was a little boy.

— Photographs tell the truth — he said and proceeded to show it to the audience. Indeed, the ochre photo clearly showed the resemblance.

Dianne was a beautiful *gringuita*, an anthropologist by profession. Eugenio looked strong, whereas don Evaristo, at 78, seemed more tired, but he was just as stubborn, rough, honest, badly spoken, and a bastard. On one of those May nights, when nephew and uncle were left alone in the large room drinking brandy, «the» conversation came up:

—What's your tool like? —Don Evaristo asked him.
—Fine —answered Eugenio, pointing at his head.

—No! —Exclaimed don Evaristo laughing—, I am asking you how big it is.

—What!? —Asked Eugenio disconcerted.

Don Evaristo, laughing his ass off, took one more sip of brandy and, putting his hand on his fly, said:

—This!

—I don't know! 9ine maybe — Eugenio managed to babble, totally confused.

—C'mon, nephew! —Exclaimed Don Evaristo, still laughing—. Translate it to centimeters!

Unable to believe what he was hearing, Eugenio began to laugh until he cried. He took two sips of brandy and said:

—I hadn't thought of that.

—Wow! — Said Don Evaristo jokingly—, mine is more prominent.

Both laughed out loud, though they knew they were exaggerating. Then Don Evaristo and Eugenio took a ceremonious shot of brandy and kept absolute silence. Eugenio knew that his uncle loved to tease people. And even more, so him, as he was such an introvert. «Always with your head in the clouds,» he used to say. So, for Eugenio, what was happening was another of his uncle's many jokes. Don Evaristo, looking at his nephew sidelong, interrupted the silence:

—I imagine, as a doctor, you must earn a lot of dollar$. According to the television, everyone is a millionaire on the other side; it is enough to see how our countrymen cross by multitudes.

—No, uncle, I'm not a millionaire or an MD —Eugenio clarified—, I'm a doctor of cosmology.

—And what's cosmology suitable for?

—Cosmology asks what the universe is made of when it came into being, how big it is.

—It is enough for me to know that we are made in the likeness of God —interrupted Don Evaristo.

— Not me! —Replied Eugenio assertively.

The room fell into a deep silence that eclipsed the seconds, which became endless. Not even the noises of the night could be heard. It was an eternity until Don Evaristo, pretending to be exhausted, broke the silence with a yawn and, without further ado, apologized and left for his bedroom. Eugenio lay on the sofa, mumbling an unfinished conversation until he fell asleep.

On the other side of the dream

He thought he saw his father and mother waving goodbye to him; although Eugenio had never met them, there were plenty of photographs in the house, and perhaps that was why he was able to identify them so clearly. Uncle Evaristo was the one who had protected him on stormy nights when he was afraid of the dark. Uncle Evaristo had always been there. And, little by little, he was entering that slumber. And he heard himself explain,

—Uncle, there was a time when it was believed that the Earth was the center of the universe until proven otherwise; in fact, our solar system sits well away from the center; it is part of the suburbs of the Milky Way. Our galaxy measures about 90,000 light-years from end to end. Of course! Light travels approximately 300,000 kilometers per second and travels a distance of 9.6 trillion kilometers in one year. Imagine the miles in 90,000 light-years. And despite its sheer size, our galaxy is an ordinary galaxy. Faced with this reality of the very large, astronomers have identified five levels of structures larger than galaxies, which they have established as clusters, aggregates, clouds, super aggregates, and super aggregates complexes. A typical group consists of a few million light-years per cubic volume of space. And it contains from 3hree to 6ix visible galaxies plus a dozen other small and as many diffuse galaxies. Our galaxy belongs to a joint group of galaxies known as the *Local* group. It is striking that the Local group contains a dominant galaxy that is not ours; Andromeda, our neighbor, is the leader. The aggregates have a diameter of 10 to 20 million light-years and contain hundreds to thousands of galaxies. Clouds come together, measure about 30 million light-years in diameter, and are joined by ropes, interestingly called *filaments* and *struts*. A typical super aggregate counts about 100 million light-years in diameter and contains approximately 10,000 galaxies. At this point, the scale makes the imagination falter, uncle. ¡ You see, super aggregates were once thought to be the most massive structures; however, they were found to be subordinate to massive walls or leaves called *super aggregate complexes*, which can expand up to a trillion light-years in diameter. But the most incredible thing, uncle, is that the Local group, ours, is on the edge of an enormous cloud called *Sculptor's Cabellera* by some and Local by others, which, in turn, is on the edge of the super-aggregate called *Virgo*.

In the other dimension, the dream.

On his way to his bedroom, Don Evaristo thought: «the surname Sotomayor now rests with Eugenio. Don't mention the surname Rubalcaba, which now rests, yes, only in Leopoldo Alejandro because his sister Ana Victoria, apparently, no longer has a chance with Eugenio. Unless he makes her his lover —Don Evaristo said laughing silently». And he liked this idea, mainly because he loved her like a daughter. He turned off the light and put his head on the pillow on one side, then pondered the possibility for a long time. In the end, he closed his eyes and fell asleep. And there, on the other side of the dream, Eugenio Leopoldo and Ana Victoria were lovers.

In this dimension, time

The next day, Don Evaristo woke up very early, got dressed as usual, and went to the kitchen, where a delicious cup of black coffee awaited him. «Sometimes dreams come true —he thought—. It would be nice to have a grandson of my son Eugenio with Ana Victoria Rubalcaba Espíndola. I see the product of that majestic, turbulent, and passionate love bear fruit of no less than my grandson: Evaristo Eugenio Sotomayor Rubalcaba. Because he would bear my name, of that, there is no doubt». And he smiled with pleasure.

Eugenio woke up when Don Evaristo gently shook his shoulder and, in a low voice, said: «Son, it's five o'clock in the morning, go up to bed.»

A dream on the other side of reality

Eugenio opened his eyes as his uncle closed the door behind him to the hallway. «The huge house is still the same —thought Eugenio— and so is hacienda Las Higueras.» Then he remembered Anna Victoria. «She is as beautiful as ever! —He exclaimed to himself as a complicit smile was drawn on his face. I like her a lot; besides, I can't forget her kisses or her caresses». And he realized that his universe gravitated in this land where the esoteric is accurate, and the real is magical-oneiric.

The reality of the other side of the dream

Eugenio opened his eyes when Dianne Odenwald kissed him, the instant the bedroom door opened to give way to a child who exclaimed:

—Mom, pop, *good morning.*
—Evaristo Eugenio, how many times have I told you to know before you open the door!?
—*Mom, I am only seven years old.*
—Come here, child, and kiss me. Ah! Your granddad does not like to be kept waiting.

And Don Evaristo was already shouting:
—Evaristo, come and ride the sorrel horse
—Coming, granddad —answered Evaristo Eugenio Sotomayor Odonwald in his little voice

180

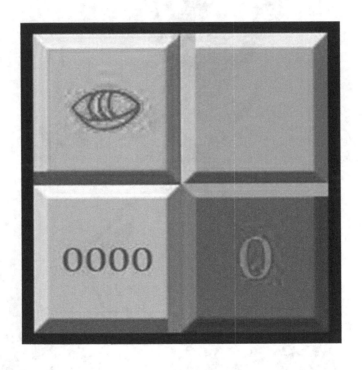

THE MEMORY OF IMAGINATION

Narrativa
© 2012 Edel Romay

NOTE AS A PRELIMINARY GUIDE

Dejà vu

«*t*o search through our labyrinths of memory, seeking for the Truth of Reality would be like searching for the Reality of Truth.» A complex search, argued my other self with itself, multiplying itself in the image of itself as an author, reader, proofreader, editor, critic, and full-time apprentice. You and I have spent all these years trying to make sense of this reflection that, without a doubt, seems esoteric to us both. At that moment, it just so happens that the author, the reader, and the publisher who inhabit, in unison, a single person ask themselves: "What is real about what we call reality?" And three voices are heard in dialogue in one real being:

— I am the other, the one who thinks, the one who sees himself reflected in me, the one who lives in Memory.
— I am the other, the one who reads you, the one who sees himself reflected in you when you write, correct, or edit.

In contrast to the others who are simultaneously in the present or the future, I am he.

— I am he, concerned with you being I in the mirror of the Mind.
— I am he, the one who engages in the blissful inner dialogue of creation.

My other I who perceives me when I write

Listen! I don't know where I read it, or maybe I'm making it up: the biochemistry of DNA in humans is a perfectible self-replica. On the other hand, I also learned that the human body is a collection of (3×10^{36}) inanimate particles. The human brain comprises 100 trillion neurons, constituting an intricate network functionally interconnected through trillions of synopses. Now, reflect, for a moment, on your existence here on planet Earth.

It is said that.

When it peered into the moon's mirror, the Reality of Truth saw only the reflection of the Truth of Reality. Position yourself in front of the mirror; the other reflects the opposite. Your right arm is his left arm.

— Whose?

—Of the other you. That is your other me.

— The Memory of past events is in the rocks — you assured me.

— The Memory of evolutionary events is trapped in DNA.

— And all this, only to remain in a perpetual present.

— The human being and nanotechnology seem to converge in the same reality.

— The whole is relative to the void and vice versa.

— Memory, after all, denotes narrative — I told myself.

And so, it happened, all of a sudden

You'll see! I was at home, in my studio, restructuring a collection of short narratives when it suddenly struck me, in the voice of Carlos Fuentes: «the thought does not die. It only measures its time». And I continued with the design I was creating. The telephone ring pulled me abruptly out of that dimension and carried me to this one. I saw it was my friend Alberto›s number and I took the call:

— Hey, have you heard already?

— No, about what?

— Carlos Fuentes just died.

— What!?

— Carlos Fuentes just died.

—!!!

— As I said, he just died.

—Alberto..., sorry..., I'm going to hang up. The news has upset me. Sorry.

The sortilege of May 15, 2012

«Déjà vu!» I said to myself as I went to tune in to the television. What›s channel 22 in Mexico? Is channel 613 here in San Francisco Bay? And Laura Barrera was announcing writer Carlos Fuentes's sudden death. I looked at the clock; it was 3:33 p.m.

The sortilege of April 19, 1998

Octavio Paz died fourteen years ago, on April 19, 1998, to be more precise. And my Mind was busy back then with story number cero, «The Refuge,» and the Kabbalistic relationship that, in my opinion, appeared to exist between the number zero and the number 9ine. As before, I still question what we call [REALITY (Reality) reality]. Coincidentally, 14 years later, I found myself in a very similar situation

May 15, 2012

It's curious, and I say it's curious because I assume that my Mind was blank since I don't remember how I got there, but I found myself in my library with a book in my hands, *Los años con Laura Díaz* by Carlos Fuentes. The clock on the wall marked 3:47 in the afternoon. I looked back at the book and leafed through it several times, stopping here or there and reading some pertinent passages aloud, until, at a given moment, I realized that I was conversing with Carlos Fuentes. Of course, his voice was there, but I was the one who spoke the most:

—I'm so sorry I was unable to converse with you. I tried several times. Maybe it was the circumstances. But things happen like this. We were out of sync. — Of course! — I learned from my wife Anita, who had spoken with Silvia Lemus, your wife, that you were on your way to London you would be out of Mexico for at least six months.

—That's right! — I was in the United States, my second home. However, my full residency is on the planet. Of course, I will explain at another time and in greater detail my concern with the latitude of the human Mind. Now I want us to be in one place: the city of Catemaco, our tangential meeting point.

«Your grandmother Emilia Boettiger Murcia and my great-aunt Maria Boettiger Murcia were sisters. María Boettiger married Uncle Domingo Álvarez Mortera, the brother of Mama Ramona Álvarez Mortera. And Mama Ramona was the mother of my mother, Maria del Carmen Gonzalez Alvarez. In other words, Maria Boettiger was also my great-aunt. But there is more: my great-grandfather, Ignacio González married Dolores Pereyra Murcia. Coincidentally, your great-grandfather Philip Boettiger Keller married Ana María Murcia, who was Dolores Pereyra Murcia's cousin no less. See! And this is the bottom of it.»

In his space-time

He woke up believing that he was still dreaming because he had no memory of having closed his eyelids at any time. He was still under this majestic tree, but he no longer spoke the universal language. «This new language is limited,» he thought because he no longer understood nature. «Before, he did, and now, he didn't,» the words resounded in his head. He thought it over again: «before..., before what? Or after what...?» The questions did not evoke an answer. But the landscape seemed the same. He closed his eyelids: «Will I be in my antepenultimate dream?» No response: «am I in my antepenultimate dream?» There was still no answer. He thought he was asleep although he was still awake; he was in that place which is neither one nor the other, that state which some call to *slumber*. At that instant, he saw himself being the epidermis between the reality out there and the reality within the self.

— The reality within? —He asked himself, somewhat confused.

— The reality of dreams —replied a voice.

— But I'm neither awake nor asleep —he replied, a little troubled.

— The physical objectivity of thought is writing —another voice intervened.

— No! The spoken word. —And he showed the cave paintings.

—*Wormholes* —answered both voices.

The very long tunnels (of the worms) went from one root to the next forming a cosmic labyrinth. "Awareness -it was said- is the fabric where each thread is the minuscule scale of [REALITY (Reality) reality], interacting on the same point. Imagination is the starting point of intentionality. The idea materializes through action. The idea is just a string that vibrates in the skein". He was in his penultimate dream. In the end, he opened his eyelids and found himself upright, contemplating in the distance. The presence was hallucinogenic: on the horizon, three enormous moon mirrors were in dialogue with each other:

— For the future, today is the past, —said one mirror.

— For the human being, today is present —added another mirror.

— For yesterday, today is the future —offered the third mirror.

[REALITY (Reality) reality]

Then he began to dig the epidermis of Memory as archaeologists do. And he only found fragments and more fragments of that reality that he was looking for. Suddenly, he witnessed something unusual and, at the same time, magnificent: imagination was stripping intelligence of the skein of reality, just at the moment when a sleeping snail woke up alone on the beach. In the next nanosecond, he witnessed the naked image of Maricielo coming out of the sea, pearled with saltwater. He sensed, so to speak, that she was the companion he had dreamt of when he was in that characteristic state of wakefulness. In that slumber or the antechamber of sleep. Where the images of reality or the reality of the pictures usually agree without prior notice from anyone. «*In a blink of an eye, we go from lightness to darkness,»* he told himself. He was in his last dream since he assumed that, perhaps, he could be part of artificial intelligence. «There is no doubt we have created *Artificial Intelligence,* but we have not yet been able to create artificial creativity,» he told himself in consolation.

In the void of the whole

He woke up, opened his eyes wide, then came the light, so suddenly denying the former reality with its radiance. However, he understood the equilateral triangulation of 3hree moon mirrors in that interval, which form a single reflection in the ignited language. In other words, the history of the future is the present, and the history of the present is the past. And the history of the past is the present future in the equilateral triangulation of 3hree moon mirrors in the exact reflection. The light had made itself present in the void of darkness.

Synopsis

At the time when humans were building language, they were also waking upward. When time discovers itself, time tries to hide in the verb with no success because you find time to conjugate the verbs. At the same time, when you find it out, it had no choice but to dance with you. «Curiously —he told himself—, there is a certain suggestive brushstroke in the silence of the imperfect subjunctive: *I/you/he/she/it/ we/you/they were...*»

In the garden, the naked tree exclaimed: «*¡La memoria Perdida del primer humano!*»
«*En el jardín el árbol desnudo exclamó*»: the lost memory of the first human.
In the garden, under the tree, the human exclaimed: «*¡La mañana del primer símbolo!*».

«En el jardín, debajo del árbol, el humano exclamó»: the morning of the first symbol!».

The pages flew.

... From one place to another without you being able to stop them. They flew like carrier pigeons. You turned your face towards me, and with your gaze, you questioned me.

— Wait! — You told me —, Where did you get such crazy ideas?
— If the tree of Knowledge exists, you are. And if you are, Eve would be. The figure is simple, just accept the conditionality we live: I am because you are.
— I insist; where did you get such crazy ideas?
—From books —I answered you and stared into the void.

«Thanks are due to the many authors I have read over the years, those dead and those alive....» Wait! What I have just told you I had already read in a book whose title, at this moment, I do not remember. The translation reads as follows: *«Las gracias van dirigidas a esos autores que he leído en el curso de todos estos años, ya sean muertos o vivos...»*

You ignored me by denying my presence. I continued to assure you that I was on the other side of the narrative:

— Wait! I'm explicitly addressing you, you on the other side of this page. And don't try to pretend you didn't understand me. The figure is simple. Of course, there's no doubt I'm addressing you. I'm going to ask you a question:

— Can you read (in brackets)?
— Yes! —You answered.
— Ok, so take a look at what I am proposing:

«The memory (within a pause) is the void. A pause (within a dream) is memory».

I stared at you, but you didn't look back at me. It's obvious you didn't understand me, or you simply didn't listen. So, I chose to ask you a second question—:

— (In brackets), Did you recognize the figure?
— Of course! —You said and set out your argument—:
«A dream (in parentheses) is Memory.
»A pause (in parentheses) is a dream.
"Memory (in parentheses) is a pause.»

This time, I think you did understand me because you observed a meditative silence while I continued arguing that the reality of dreams is found in Memory (in parentheses). Simply said, because Memory is a quantum reality (in parentheses). Besides, I tell you, Memory is illusory (in parentheses).

Memory is elusive

—Memory is a tree whose most juicy fruit is imagination.
—Writing is a matter of stubbornness, but publishing is a matter of luck.
—I agree.
—I am going to tell you a "story" that I had some time ago.
—You mean a dream —you corrected me.
—In this particular case, a story is a dream —I replied.

Link:

And I went on to reveal to you, in 3 parts, a sketch of what was a dreamt story:

Sketch 1: In Miguel de Cervantes Saavedra's dream, the reality of Galilea is at the intersection between the *Idioma español* and the English language.

Sketch 2: In William Shakespeare's dream, the reality of Galilea is at the intersection of the English language with the *Idioma español*.

Sketch 3: In the dream of Galilea, the reality of Miguel and William is in the *Southwest*, that is, in the Southwest of the United States.

A suggestive stroke: Galilea was a young woman with a simply monumental, tanned body. Intelligent, cheerful, independent, and audacious. At 26, she obtained her doctorate in comparative literature from the University of California at Berkeley. Despite Galilea's young age, she had traveled almost all over the world; due to her parents' profession: one devoted to theoretical Physics, the other to archaeology. Galilea grew up speaking English and *español* simultaneously

The plot of a short story like a dream

Galilea left the bathroom naked, wiping her well-molded, turgid pair of breasts with a towel, thinking she was still dreaming. She stopped for a second and went to the bedroom to check if she was still sleeping. But, to her surprise, she did not find herself in the bedroom. The bed only bore the appearance that someone had slept there. And she thought, «If I'm not in the bedroom, I might be in the study.» And I was in the studio writing at the same time as I was reading myself, paying close attention to punctuation:

"the pencil has been present in the unfolding of my manuscripts. —Galilea emphasized *manuscripts*—. Pencil and pen are an extension of my fingers. My fingers are an extension of my Mind. Imagination is an annex to my Mind. In short, my reflective self is the genesis of my realization through my manuscripts because, despite the digital world in which I exist today, wherever I may be, I still make notes in pencil."

All this happened in a nanosecond because when Galilea dropped the pencil on the ground, it was apparent that she was in Solano Cellars, conversing with Miguel and William. The three of them were drinking red wine.

—Do you like red wine? —Asked William.
—Yes! As much as I like to read a good book —responded Galilea.
—Ummm —said William.
—A visual acoustic —exclaimed the waitress, who could not understand what she was witnessing.

By the way, Solano Cellars is in Albany, California.

Here, the reality; over there, time.

«Time invents itself when it is in this reality,» *revealed* the author, reader, proofreader, editor, and critic combined. And you are naturally the narrative within this real fiction that is developing. That is, description and redrafting come together so that you and I can exist in the same space-time.

The plot of a dream like a short story

Galilea awakened a little later than usual. She stretched like a feline as if looking for the perfect fit of her body. Finally, she jumped up and went to the bathroom. There, under the shower, she could mentalize the dream, then, excited with her inner conversation, she came out, towel in hand, drying her titties. She took her robe and headed for the kitchen to make herself a cup of black coffee. The aroma of the coffee greeted her while she savored it in no hurry. Satisfied, she left the kitchen for the studio, picked up the pencil from the floor, placed the cup of coffee on the desk, and, on a blank sheet of paper, wrote: «The night chased the day until it caught up with the dawn. In one kiss, the night yielded the day in the coitus at twilight. The day chased the night until it caught up to nightfall. In a kiss, the day yielded to the night in the coitus at twilight».

Galilea did not know in what dream she was; the images were so suggestively authentic that she might well have assured, without a doubt, that she was awake. You and I are the only witnesses of the following dialogue:

—Why poetry? —Asked William.
—To look for 5ive sugar islands —responded Miguel— which, it is assumed, navigate through a vast sea of salt sitting on that score.

Galilea opened and closed her eyelids as if to make sure she was awake. She continued writing: «I dream in a dream *soñando que* I dream in a dream *soñando*…That is, the light that darkens in the light that darkens in the darkness of the light that darkens in the light that I believe I see in the distance that I am perceiving… I dream in a light that I dream *soñando que* I dream in a light that I dream *soñando in the light. Despierto que despierto* from a dream *que soñando* I dream in a dream *que despierto soñando*… I wake up from a dream that I am awaked *soñando que despierto* from a dream in a dream soñando….»

Galilea gradually vanished behind the pencil that, in the end, fell on the blank sheet of paper. In this new reality, Galilea witnessed the dialogue that took place between the pencil and the blank piece of paper:

— The reality of dreams is found in Memory's fantasy —said the blank piece of paper.
— The manuscript format is in quantum geometry —the pencil responded.

(In parentheses)

In that precise instant in which your eyes are opening, the imagination decided to morph into Galilea. Already in the form of a woman, the vision agreed to undress completely. Do you see her? You have to admit that Galilea is a gorgeous woman.

— Come on! You remind me of Paul Ricoeur — my imagination warned me.
— Why? —I asked, surprised.

And at that very moment, the inevitable happened: Paul Ricoeur intervened:

—Poetry goes right to the essence of action precisely because it ties together **muthos** and **mimēsis**, that is, in our vocabulary, fiction, and description.

Then, Galilea, dancing, jocose and provocative, paraphrased in Spanish:

—La poesía va directo a la esencia de la acción precisamente porque enlaza **muthos** y **mimēsis**, es decir, en nuestro vocabulario, ficción y readscripción—. At first, it was darkness, the vast immensity of the void. In the beginning, it was the number *zero*, that is to say, the black matter of the void. At first, it was *nothing*. And the spontaneous action of nothingness produced a luminous dot (*a dot* ●) in the darkness of the *whole's* void. The forum was floodlit in the semidarkness of the landscape. An instant in which two voices are heard screaming: «the information, the conformation, the deformation, the transformation of a sphere into cubits is the projection of a circle into tiny squares.» Could you wait a minute and let me explain? There is only one tree in the garden. There is only one book underneath the tree, whose pages the wind blows tirelessly over and over again. In the end, the book remains open on page 9ine, and just then, it discovers itself and begins to reread itself. I remember the early morning vividly when I was arriving at the town by the Royal road. The half-dark dawn, which may well have been the half-dark dusk, drew shadows in the forest as my horse trotted along the route. Those shadows were diffuse; as far as I could see, one materialized in front of me, and, raising his voice, he said to me: «My name is Segunda,» while the other shadow intervened: «My name is Última.» I was surprised, not so my horse, which only gazed into the distance. After a moment, I could clearly distinguish that Segunda was a beautiful young light brunette and that Última was a gorgeous young redhead. Both are dress in the colors of the sky and sea. Just then, the dialogue took place:

—Nothing is real without an observer —said Última.
—*Nada es real sin un observador —dijo Segunda.*
—Nothing is real without evidence —said Última.
—*Nada es real sin evidencia —dijo Segunda.*
—Nothing is everything —said Última.
—*Nada es todo —dijo Segunda.*
—Evidence —a perfect marriage between science and faith —said Última.
—*Evidencia, un perfecto casamiento entre la ciencia y la fe —dijo Segunda.*
—Imagination versus intelligence —I intervened.
—No! Intelligence and imagination is the mirror of human reality —they exclaimed

In the twilight

The garden ceased to be a garden once the human awakened. The human only saw on the horizon a naked tree that asked the sea and the sky to fill its arms with sheets of paper. In the distance, the wind played with the reflection of the sea and the sky. In the mirror of the horizon, it seemed that sea and sky were uniting when, suddenly, they said:

—The equation of I «*soy yo*» —Said the mirror.

—You are I, as I am you, in the reflection of water —replied Maricielo.

Under a bare tree, a book flicks through itself, leafing through its pages. At the next glance, he thought he saw the presence of a human figure trying to get off the page of a future book, which is about to be written.

Wait! Listen! It is the voice of Octavio Paz:

Creció en mi frente un árbol.
Creció hacia adentro.
Sus raíces son venas,
nervios sus ramas,
sus confusos follajes pensamientos.

A tree grew inside my head
A tree grew in
Its roots are veins
Its branches nerves
Thoughts its tangled foliage

[REALITY (Reality) reality]

He slowly opened his eyelids and could immediately recognize that he was in the middle of the sea of a sheet of white paper. Then he saw one blank sheet of paper resting on an antique cedar desk. He could see on the horizon that the library was overflowing with books. In the middle of a blank sheet of paper, a drop of ink attached to a word shouted your name.

In the following immediate reality

He slowly opened his eyelids and found himself in the middle of the sea with a sheet of cybernetic white paper. The blank sheet of paper was the image of a traditional sheet of paper in a digital program (Word). The library was on the Cybernet. On the sheet of cybernetic paper, a pulse is connected to a word that exclaimed your name.

Refraction of the image

At the bottom of a crystalline pond, a mirror vainly sought a reflection of itself. «In water, mirrors are liquid,» said a fish moving in and out of the reflection.

A mirage over the horizon of time

Finally, he opened his eyelids, and, with a single thought, the mirage of the horizon reflected his face, which was made of traditional paper, with conventional ink. It was a conventional book resting on an ancient standard desk abandoned in a digital world, to his surprise. And what he believed to be his eyes were, in truth, the eyes of the reader. The symbiosis was evident; he read because she was reading it. And in doing so, the narrative flowed clearly into both their minds. The book outlined the passage of the traditional human through an old-fashioned world that no longer existed. It was a matter of a moment. The coitus had happened; then, the book ceased to exist. Galilea abandoned it in sleep. Maricielo is in the antechamber where the possibility of materializing into a future author and reader was observed. As it was put by Carlos Fuentes: «I am always thinking about the first reader of a future book, a reader who is not yet born and who will discover my work in fifty years.»

Mirror-image

It is the mirror that reflects itself. And so, it was that the human was reflected on the cybernetic quantum entity on the other side of the mirror, took note in his language, and archived the find as an archaeological artifact:

«The human is the first state of communication with the WHOLE.»
«The dream is the second state of communication with the mind.»
«The mind is the third state of communication with the cosmos.»
«The cosmos is the fourth state of communication with the vacuum.»
«The VOID is the fifth reflective state of mind.»

Genesis

Maricielo was still inside the tunnel, witnessing the first cave paintings on the walls of the cave. The possibility of manifesting herself in a future time was being measured, precisely, in the duality of quantum physics. However, at one point, the holes opened into corridors and passageways where the ropes vibrated, creating, from one nanosecond to the subsequent, unified realities. That is to say, the threads of the strings formed knots announcing the critical passage of the matter, structuring complex networks of fabrics. Afterward, a tunnel opened through which Maricielo was transported to the bottom of a cave. There, in the semidarkness of the tunnel, she heard the voice of Carlos Fuentes: « Maricielo! The book begins when it is finished».

The city of Berkeley, 2062

On May 15, Elizabeth Stuart surprised her boyfriend with an uncommon gift.

—My love —she said—, open it, I long to say your face.
—You are scaring me, Eli —he answered as he opened the package.

All it took was a glance at the cover for Carlos Cifuentes' face to light up.

— This is extraordinary, my love, a compendium of the posthumous works of Carlos Fuentes.
—Yes, my love! I read your Mind!

And they kissed tenderly. It was a Friday night, and they were having dinner at the Chez Panisse Restaurant at 1519 Shattuck Ave., between Cedar St. and Vine St. in Berkeley. They had finally decided the date of their marriage. Carlos flipped through the traditional printed book several times until Eli, holding his hand, said to him:

— Also, I give you this traditional pencil with which.
— Of course! — Carlos interrupted her as she wrote a special note inside the book.

In fact

On September 9inth, 2012, Maricielo Deneuve Álvarez, daughter of French chef Marcel Denueve Arnaud and essayist and poet Mónica Álvarez Vitti, was born in the city of Xalapa (Veracruz, Mexico).

On April 15teenth, 2034, the concert pianist Maricielo Denueve Álvarez married the cosmologist Francisco Cifuentes Cienfuegos, in Mexico City.

On May 4ourth, 2037, his beloved son Carlos Cifuentes Deneuve was born. Fortunately, thanks to his parent's profession, Carlos had the opportunity to know the world's great and beautiful cities. However, he was educated, mainly in the United States of America.

On April 22ond, 2064, the doctor of Theoretical Physics married Archaeology Elizabeth Stuart in Berkeley. Carlos Cifuentes Deneuve was 33 years old and Eli 27 years old. Obviously, for reasons of their professions, they were postponing having children. Until one day, they lost control, and Eli became pregnant. So, on February 14ourteenth, 2068, his beloved daughter Galilea Cifuentes Stuart was born in Berkeley.

The city of Berkeley, 2092

On May 15teenth, 2092, searching among the relics of his father, that is, in the traditional library, he found the volume of posthumous works by Carlos Fuentes, opened the cover, and carefully read the dedication:

«Honey, I love you more than ever, Eli. 5-15-2062»
«My love, I have not words with which to express how much I love you...».

Galilea began to devour the traditional letters, of the conventional volume, in the traditional library, with the same eagerness as her parents did thirty years ago.

Printed in the United States
by Baker & Taylor Publisher Services